A TALENT FOR MURDER

by Anna Mary Wells

"The book carries an amazing impact of reality, probably because of its expert pacing and exceptional characterization. Her people, some pretty far off the normal beam, are set down with a good deal of insight and care, and come through with flying colors."
—*Detroit Free Press*

Titles by Anna Mary Wells available in Perennial Library

A TALENT

FOR

Murder

BY

A N N A   M A R Y   W E L L S

PERENNIAL LIBRARY
Harper & Row, Publishers
New York, Cambridge, Hagerstown, Philadelphia, San Francisco
London, Mexico City, São Paulo, Sydney

The characters and situations in this work are wholly fictional and imaginary, and do not portray and are not intended to portray any actual persons or parties.

A hardcover edition of this book was originally published by Alfred A. Knopf, Inc. It is here reprinted by arrangement.

First PERENNIAL LIBRARY edition published 1981.

ISBN: 0-06-080535-8

81 82 83 84 85 10 9 8 7 6 5 4 3 2 1

A TALENT FOR MURDER

Chapter 1

Dr. Hillis Owen studied the oblong cardboard "new patient" form with a little frown of concentration. Miss Pomeroy, standing respectfully at his left elbow, knew perfectly well what was wrong with it, he felt sure, but it was no use appealing to her for help until he had pinned down for himself what it was about it that seemed odd. Suddenly he had it. Flipping the card away from him across the polished desk, he leaned back in his swivel chair and laughed aloud at Pomeroy.

"Tell her I'm not that kind of a psychiatrist," he said.

Pomeroy looked blank. She was playing dumb today.

"I haven't time to sit around courtrooms twiddling my thumbs," he went on impatiently. "Go tell her to find somebody else to explain to the jury that she wasn't responsible when everything went blank and she pulled that little tiny trigger."

"The trial is over, Dr. Owen," Miss Pomeroy replied politely. "Mrs. Meredith was acquitted."

3

"I'm still not interested." Pomeroy was always putting him in the wrong. That woman knew entirely too much. Invaluable office nurse, but irritating to have around all the time.

"I'll tell her you can't be of assistance to her in any legal difficulty," she said, not moving toward the door, "but what shall I say if she still wants to come in?"

"What does she look like, Pomeroy?" Dr. Owen folded his hands behind his head and grinned the engaging, boyish grin that put his most difficult patients at their ease.

"Very much like the newspaper photographs, doctor."

"Mmmm. Mostly legs. Does she have a full complement of other parts?"

"I should call her a very good looking woman—girl, if I didn't know who she was."

"Is it a game, or does she really need to see me?"

"I think she's in trouble, doctor."

Dr. Owen sighed. Miss Pomeroy, with her neatly waved gray hair, and her pink, sensible face above an always spotless uniform was the voice of his conscience, his guidepost to rectitude as well as his office nurse. A very wise old lady, he told his patients sometimes, but none of them appreciated her as he did.

"I've never been in the confidence of a murderess, Pomeroy. I'm not sure I'll know what to say. D'you think it's safe?"

"I think so, doctor."

"Very well then, show her in, but keep a police whistle handy."

It wasn't a very good joke, and Dr. Owen was surprised

to find that he was actually a little nervous as he waited to see Mrs. Jerome Meredith.

She came in quietly through the heavy door and moved almost soundlessly across the thick carpet. She was a pretty woman, smaller than he had expected, quietly dressed and inconspicuous. You wouldn't notice her in a crowd unless the memory of her picture on the front of a tabloid newspaper was very fresh in your mind. Her dark hair framed a square, pale little face on which a few freckles stood out sharply.

Dr. Owen stood up, smiling his new patient smile, and held out his right hand. The one she gave him was small and black gloved, and her clasp was firm. She didn't look neurotic, he noted professionally. Her eyes were steady but not fixed; the pallor of her face indicated strain, but she was fully mistress of herself. Too much control; when she had to let go the effects would be disastrous. Her voice was low, throaty and pleasant.

"I suppose you know who I am, Dr. Owen. It's too soon to hope to meet anyone who doesn't."

"I hope you aren't counting on that," he told her, "for you'll be surprised. Right now I'll bet more people could identify Adolf Hitler than Doris Meredith. And in a month—pouf. There's a lot of news to put on front pages these days."

Although he spoke lightly he was watching her narrowly. It would be a help to know from the start how well she really liked the notoriety.

She laughed without a shade of annoyance that he could detect crossing her face.

"That's very comforting, doctor."

"Wait and see. You'll probably be disappointed."

"Maybe." She considered the idea without anger. "I see what you mean, but I really think I'll be glad to be anonymous again. However, you never know what you are going to feel about things, do you?"

"Seldom," he agreed. He always tried to like his patients; a psychiatrist needed sympathy in order to work effectively, but it irritated him to note how easy it was going to be to like Mrs. Meredith. She was probably playing her tricks on him, and he was proving as susceptible as a juryman.

She braced herself slightly but visibly, and came to the point.

"Your knowing who I am is a help, for it's about my— recent trouble I want to see you. I understand that anything I tell you in a consultation is in confidence."

"Wait a minute," he said sharply. "The answer to that one is yes and no. My oath as a physician pledges me to serve your best interests and not to gossip about what I find out incidentally to that service. But I'm not sworn to secrecy like a priest. Society's interest comes first for me, as a physician, and yours comes second. For example, suppose I have a wealthy and highly respected patient who's a secret drug addict. I don't have to go around blasting his reputation by indiscriminate gossip, but I do have to report the facts to the proper authorities. If you tell me anything that's legally incriminating I shall have to do the same thing. Don't come here looking for a confessional."

Her pale face flushed at his tone. She sat quietly considering what he had said for a moment before she answered. It was a rare compliment; few social acquaintances and almost no patients waited until he had finished speaking to formulate an answer. She spoke at last, thoughtfully.

"I think my legal position is unassailable," she said. "I was acquitted, you know, and I don't believe I can be tried again for that crime, regardless of what I say or do. I'm not quite certain; my lawyer was my brother, and I didn't want to ask him, for I knew it would distress him very much to find that I think I need the services of a psychiatrist. I believe I run very little risk in what I tell you, and that little I'm willing to chance."

He nodded without speaking.

"Dr. Owen, I don't know whether or not I shot my husband," she said.

The hands folded in her lap tightened, and she visibly swallowed a lump in her throat; her voice was urgent, but still quiet and controlled. A good psychiatrist doesn't show surprise. Dr. Owen looked at her without any change of expression.

"You didn't plead insanity as your defense?"

"Oh, no, it was never remotely suggested."

"Perhaps you'd better tell me the whole story—everything. I didn't follow your trial."

She sighed and began as if she were reciting a lesson.

"On the night of December 3rd 1940 I went to the theater with my brother. The play was *Arsenic and Old Lace*; the newspapers made a good deal of the fact that it was a mystery drama just like—like mine." She put her handkerchief to her lips and made a little sound that could have been a laugh or a sob or a cough.

"Look," he said kindly. "You have rather a long story to tell me. It will be easier if you cut the histrionics. I know it's hard after all those weeks before a jury, but try. Afterwards you may want to break down and cry; if I think it will do you good I'll tell you to go ahead. Meanwhile try to tell it to me just as a case history. Forget that it's a good story."

She nodded.

"During the first intermission I went into a drug store near the theater to telephone home. I had a new nursemaid with my little girl, and I wanted to know if the child had gone off to sleep happily with her. I couldn't get any answer at my apartment. I rang two or three times, and then I was frightened. Both my husband and the nursemaid should have been at home. We lived at 427 East 52nd Street, and we were at a theater on West 45th. I came out of the drug store, hailed a taxi, and had myself driven home."

"And your brother?"

"I didn't wait to find him. I should have, of course. I suppose I was a little panicky. The taxi drove directly to the apartment. I've never been able to remember the route, but there were no serious traffic obstructions, and he must have gone a more or less usual way or I should have remembered. I wouldn't remember the driver, but I have seen him—frequently—since."

"Just a minute now, Mrs. Meredith. You say you don't know whether or not you shot your husband. Is your memory entirely clear on the points you are covering now?"

"Entirely, except as to my motives. Different ones were later ascribed to me. As to action, though, I'll tell you when I come to the place where there is any doubt. I'm almost there. I was in a hurry—anxious about the baby, but then, if nothing were wrong I wanted to get back to the theater with as little delay as possible so as not to alarm my brother. I watched the meter and had the change counted out by the time the taxi stopped. I opened the car door and ran into the building. We have an automatic elevator at 427, and no doorman. I went up to the apartment without meeting anyone, and let myself in. There's a big entrance foyer that can be used as a dining room. The kitchen and a dropped living room are to the right, the bedrooms and bath to the left."

She stopped short.

"Now comes the difficult part," she went on, more slowly. "I'd better tell you first the official version—the story on the basis of which I was acquitted—the one I hope is true."

The effort she was making appeared to be rather for concentration than for control. She spoke slowly, like a person feeling her way in the dark, no longer reciting a lesson.

"My husband, I supposed, was in the living room. But I didn't go in there at all—didn't even look in. I tiptoed past. I suddenly realized that he would think this ultra-maternal attitude ridiculous—and I was afraid of surprising him in an awkward predicament."

She laughed, a strained little laugh.

"After all, he had expected to be alone for the evening. He wasn't answering the telephone. I was safely out of the way at a theater. It's not a very graceful position—the wronged wife returning suddenly."

"You thought he was entertaining a woman?"

"I was almost sure he was. I tiptoed into the nursery. Adriana was asleep, and so was her nurse. Everything was in order—the room well aired, the child warmly covered. I was still troubled, of course, to think that Miss Wright slept so soundly the telephone couldn't waken her, but it didn't seem enough to keep me at home when my brother was waiting. I went directly out—I think I went directly out."

"Your husband didn't hear you enter or leave?"

"My husband was probably dead."

"Still, not knowing that at the time, didn't you think it odd he didn't hear you and call out?"

"I was being very quiet. And at the time his silence seemed another reason for thinking there might be someone with him."

"Yes. Go on, then."

"I went back downstairs, and the taxi was waiting. I hadn't told him to, but he said I'd seemed in such a hurry he thought likely I'd be coming out again in a minute. I told him to take me back to the theater, and he did."

"And your brother?"

"He'd very sensibly gone back in at the end of the intermission. I had the stub of my own ticket; I was holding it when we first went in. I got back in without making much disturbance. And then I did a very foolish thing. I didn't want a lot of explaining, so I whispered that I'd had a headache, bought some aspirin and coffee, and sat still in the drug store, over the coffee, until the aspirin began to work. It was a silly little lie. I worried about Miss Wright so much I didn't follow the last two acts very closely. And afterwards I pled the headache again to go straight home. Dick was tired and wouldn't come up."

"Dick is your brother?"

"Yes. I went into the living room alone, and found Jerome sitting in his favorite chair with blood and brains spattered everywhere."

She closed her eyes for a moment, and then said, in a more natural voice: "It's such a relief to tell it to you like that. For months I've been saying I found him 'with a bullet through his head.' It sounds better. People haven't any idea what it means. Have you ever seen a man who had been shot in the head?"

"Yes," Dr. Owen said. "I've seen worse than that. I've seen men die in a number of unpleasant ways. A medical student gets over minding before he takes his degree."

"Yes, of course," she said. "It was the second violent death I had discovered, but the other wasn't—messy."

"The second?"

"My father committed suicide in 1929. An overdose of the medicine he was taking for a heart condition. He must have thought that that way we couldn't be sure, but we were. Father didn't make mistakes."

She paused again to organize her thoughts. "I'm sorry

I'm rambling," she said. "I called Dick at once, but he hadn't reached home yet. He has an apartment in town, but that night he went out to our mother's home in West-chester. I kept trying his apartment and he didn't answer. I somehow didn't think of the police. I got him at last at the Westchester house, and he told me to call the police at once. They got here before he did. He brought mother along to look after me and the baby. But now I'd better go back. What I've just told you is what I told on the witness stand. But the prosecutor told another story. I had to sit there and listen to it, of course. And now I'm not sure. I dream it both ways. I don't know which I remember."

"The first step toward clearing it up is to tell me what the prosecutor said."

"He said that I had somehow learned that Jerome had an assignation that evening in our apartment—it came out, later on, that Miss Wright had been drugged—that I'd gone home between the acts to confront him, that I found him with a woman, and shot him."

Hillis Owen chose to ignore the mounting hysteria in her voice.

"The woman?" he inquired in a matter-of-fact manner.

"None was named. That was a weakness in his case. If she existed, she's never turned up to accuse me."

"It would be awkward for her of course," the doctor said thoughtfully, and then smiled. "Excuse me if I seem dull witted. Detective work's out of my field."

"You mean to brand me a murderess she'd have had to brand herself an adulteress, or whatever they call them nowadays? I suppose so, though the way people regard such things, it doesn't seem as if that would be enough to keep her from telling, does it?"

"But you—how do you remember her?"

"If you were a detective or a lawyer I couldn't tell you," she answered. "That's one reason I didn't give up and confess all this before. It's not fair to involve an innocent woman in my hallucinations, if that's what they are. If I saw a woman there, it was Ruth Granger."

"You know her?"

"She was my husband's mistress."

"You are certain?"

"Quite. I'd known it for a long time."

"And how did you feel about it?"

She shrugged her shoulders.

"It wasn't a very happy marriage, but as marriages go, I dare say it was average. We had a lot in common. We enjoyed each other's company. We both loved Adriana. I miss him," she said, and her eyes suddenly brimmed with tears. She wiped them away quickly, with a small, untrimmed white handkerchief. "Dick has been warning me I mustn't do that," she explained. "It would be too obvious a play for the jury, crying over him. I couldn't even wear black at the trial."

"Let's get back to the night of December 3rd," Hillis said. "What were they doing when you came in?"

"She was in his arms."

"In the chair where you later found him dead?"

"No, on the sofa. When they saw me, they both stood up."

"And then?"

"I—I laughed, and said something about melodrama. And then I went into my own room to give them a chance to compose themselves—and to get the gun."

"Whose gun was it?"

"Jerome's. He kept it in his second bureau drawer, under his socks. I powdered my nose very calmly, and took it out. When I went back, Jerome was sitting in his chair, and Ruth was standing by the window. They were both smoking. Jerome said: 'It strikes me this is in rather bad taste, Doris,' and I shot him."

"And Miss Granger?"

"Didn't even wait to see if he were dead. She ran. I heard her slam the door and hoped she hadn't waked the baby."

"What about her coat and hat?"

"I can't remember. They must have been lying on a chair in the hall where she could snatch them up—but I don't recall seeing them. After the door slammed, I looked in the nursery—still carrying the gun. Then I wiped it off with a towel and put it on the floor and came away."

"Your husband died instantly?"

"He had time to say: 'Don't.' "

"This brother you speak of"—Hillis was puzzled. "Do you mean that the same brother who was with you at the time defended you at your trial?"

"Yes. It was unusual, but not unheard of. All Dick's lawyer friends advised us against it, but he wanted to, and it seems he was right."

"But he was a witness himself?"

"Yes, but the law makes large allowances for criminals, you know. A man can even defend himself."

"Let me see if I have this straight now," Dr. Owen said thoughtfully. "Whatever you did at the apartment, you immediately afterward left the building and returned to the theater in the same taxi you had used to come from it?"

"That's right."

"And all during the last act you were abstracted—thinking about Miss Wright, and whether she was going to be competent to take care of your baby?"

"Or about having murdered my husband and whether I was going to be able to escape hanging."

"One or the other. I see. And after the theater you went directly home in another taxi?"

"We were in my brother's car then."

Dr. Owen narrowed his eyes and drummed his fingers on the desk.

"The gun?"

"Was on the floor in the living room. Fingerprints had been wiped off. It was Jerome's."

"How about suicide?"

"The experts thought not. Angle of incidence and powder burns and position of the gun. I'm afraid I didn't understand it all."

"Well then, what next?"

"I stayed in the baby's room until the police came. I didn't want her frightened if the disturbance wakened her."

"And when did you find that your memory of the events

of that evening was confused?"

"I'm not sure." She rubbed her forehead wearily. "I went over and over my story with Dick. He made me act out everything I'd done—everything I was going to say I'd done—so it wouldn't sound as if I were repeating it by rote. And he kept telling me what the prosecutor would say. And then I was in the witness stand, and I didn't know which was right."

"But you said nothing of this to anyone, and continued to tell the story in which your brother had coached you?"

She flushed quickly, but kept her temper, and Dr. Owen was ashamed of baiting her.

"That's right," she said.

"And what did Miss Granger do?"

"Mrs. Granger. She had an alibi that was never called into question. She had spent the evening with her husband at their home on Long Island."

"And you've never discussed your uncertainty with your brother?"

"No, never."

"Does he believe in your innocence?"

"I think so. I'm almost certain. If he has a doubt, I'm sure he represses it."

"But, Mrs. Meredith, there's a much simpler way than psychoanalysis to find the answer to your question. Mrs. Granger must know whether or not she saw you shoot your husband. Why don't you ask her?"

"Do you suppose I haven't thought of that? What reason have I for thinking that she would answer me truthfully—that she wouldn't jump at the chance to torture me with my uncertainty? It's not a secret I dare share with anyone. Listening to her testimony, I used to try and try to see into her mind, to guess where she was telling the truth and where she was lying. But I never could at all."

Dr. Owen nodded.

"I see. But still, why come to me? You've been under a terrible strain; your mind is defending itself from the consequences. Now that it's all over and you're free to carry on your life as you choose, there's every reason to suppose that the scars will heal, or, to use a more precise analogy, the defenses crumble. I'm supposing, brutally, that you did kill your husband. If you did, it's a merciful thing for a woman like you that you can't remember. Why not let well enough alone?"

"Because of the future. I have no masochistic ideas about doing penance for my sins, Dr. Owen. If I killed Jerome, that's past, and there's nothing I can do. But there's Adriana. Jerome's people have her now. I want her back, but only if I'm sure I'm fit to have her. If I'm insane I want to know it and be protected against myself."

He stood up and walked to the window. His reluctance to undertake this case astonished him. It should be a fascinating study, and yet his mind revolted from it.

"You understand, if I accept you as a patient, Mrs. Meredith, you will have to follow through wherever my findings may lead? There's no turning back half way."

"I understand," she said, half rising and sinking back into the chair, her pallor increasing. "You—you think I did it, Dr. Owen. You think I'm insane."

"Wait a minute, young lady," he said lightly, resuming his professional air of reassurance. "You've been associating too much with lawyers. The scientific mind doesn't jump to conclusions in any such hasty fashion. I have no idea whether or not you're insane. So far I've seen nothing to indicate that you are, but then I haven't started yet. But if we go into this thing together, I want you to realize now the worst that can happen."

"Commitment to an asylum. Is that so very bad, doctor?"

"Not bad at all for anyone who can take it philosophically. Few can, of course. You have some private means?"

"Why, yes, a small income." She looked bewildered at the change of subject.

"Excellent. The public institutions are good enough; the best private ones are splendid. You associate with people like yourself—and you'd be surprised how many patients are educated, amusing people like you. You're protected from association with the others. You're encouraged to develop your talents—writing, music, drawing, sculpture, sewing, what have you. You have books and music, good plays, good food, outdoor exercise, a simple, wholesome life. It's the Greek ideal—nothing to excess."

"Why are you telling me all this, doctor, unless you believe it's what's going to happen to me?"

"I can get on better with my investigation if I can remove some of the dread of the worse alternative. It's the truth I'm telling, incidentally."

"All right," she said.

"Very well, then," he answered. "We go ahead. We left you in your daughter's room waiting for the police."

"They were very kind and polite that night," she said. "Everyone was protecting me—the shock. Dick and mother came soon after the police. They had tried to waken Miss Wright and question her. It was hard to get her awake, and they drove her into hysterics and took her to police headquarters and the doctor there found out she'd been drugged with a mild sedative. She swore she hadn't taken any knowingly. They badgered her—but you want to know about me. I'm sorry. Everything was confused. Dick talked to the police. And of course he told them my story about the aspirin. There hadn't been time for me to tell him the truth, you see. The apartment was full of people milling around. Jerome's family came, and they were all crying and asking questions too. Finally mother took me and the baby home for the night."

"Where was that?"

"To Westchester."

"And when were you arrested?"

"The taxi-driver read about the murder in the morning paper, and went right to headquarters. They didn't think, at first, that I might have been the woman. But when they found out they arrested me at once."

"But if you'd murdered your husband you must have realized that the aspirin story was awfully thin. You're an intelligent woman."

"I didn't know taxi-drivers paid that much attention to their fares. But anyway, if I did kill him it was on impulse, and I cooked up that story for Dick in a hurry."

"On the other hand, if you didn't kill him, where did your idea about the other woman originate?"

"As we were leaving for the theater I thought I saw Ruth sitting in a car parked at the curb. It was just a glimpse; I wasn't even sure, but it was enough to start the chain of thought. You see, whichever way I remember it, the idea of the woman is there."

"Yes," he said, "and how did you react to that idea? Even if you can't remember what happened in the apartment, you ought to know what your motives and intentions were."

"I know I didn't plan it. My purpose in going home— my conscious purpose, at least—was to see Adriana. But I do remember feeling dreadfully upset all during the last two acts of the play—more upset than it seems now I should have felt over Betty Wright's very mild defection."

"Were you jealous? Had you quarrelled with your husband over this woman?"

"No, never. I made a point of not quarrelling. I suppose I was jealous although I tried not to show it, tried not even to feel it. Jerome wanted to be modern and I tried to please him."

"I think that will be all for today, Mrs. Meredith. Make an appointment for next week with Miss Pomeroy as you leave. And Mrs. Meredith—one further word of warning. If you're sane and killed him, I'm going to have you committed anyway. For in that case you're much too clever to be running around loose."

Chapter 2

Dr. Owen rated the opinions of Miss Pomeroy among the most valuable of the data on which he based his conclusions about his patients. Not that Miss Pomeroy employed the scientific method—quite the contrary, in fact; she went in for snap judgments and she maintained them. And in an astonishingly large percentage of cases, the facts maintained them too. He confided in her discretion even more completely than in her judgment, and had no professional secrets from her. It was without any qualm, therefore, that he said to her later in the afternoon, when he had finished seeing patients:

"That Meredith woman's got the damnedest story I ever heard."

Miss Pomeroy, who was a Methodist, stiffened a little at the profanity.

"Sorry, Pomeroy," he laughed, "but it really is. I'll bet you'd say so yourself. She claims she doesn't know whether or not she shot her husband."

"Dreadful," Miss Pomeroy said succinctly.

"I've consented to work with her," he said, "but I think I'm a little sorry already. I start off with a prejudice against lady murderesses who can't remember."

"Mrs. Meredith was acquitted," Miss Pomeroy said stiffly.

"But I'm no jury," Hillis rejoined moodily. "And you can see for yourself, Pomeroy, the chances are all against her. If she did it, there's plenty of reason for her subconscious to build up a defense. If she didn't, and is otherwise as normal as she seems, there's practically no reason for her to be confused. What sort of a plea did that brother of hers make?"

"Wonderful. The papers were full of it. He had the jury in tears, and the *Times* said that even the judge blew his nose rather suspiciously."

Trust Pomeroy to have all the crime news at her respectable fingertips! It was she who had pointed out to Dr. Owen that the *Times* was the paper to read if you really wanted all the gory details of a revolting story.

"With all those pictures and the little tiny pages there really isn't room for much information in the tabloids. The *Times* headlines may throw you off, of course, but continued on page 68 you can usually find things no less respectable paper would dare to print."

"Well, if she didn't do it she's been the victim of a diabolical piece of suggestion. I'd like to know whether or not it was deliberate. And of course her brother was in the best position to plant it. Was he trying to have her acquitted or did he slip up? What had he to gain if he'd sent her to the chair?"

"He's her twin brother, doctor," Miss Pomeroy said in a horrified tone. "They're devoted to one another."

"Would he get her money if she died?"

"The papers never said anything about that, but I shouldn't think so. She's married and has a child."

He laughed and shrugged. "Anyway, I'm a doctor, not a detective. What I find out I'll have to find out from

Mrs. Meredith herself. But I'd still like to work it so I could get a gander at that guy."

"The *Times* said his argument was brilliantly reasoned as well as emotionally powerful."

"So she comes of a brilliant family, does she?" The doctor lit a cigarette, and bit down so hard on it that he cut it in two, and had to throw it away and start another. "The worst part of the business to me is that I can't get over feeling she's pulling my leg. But why? I don't see anything she has to gain."

"Perhaps you've let yourself be prejudiced by her record, doctor."

The subject of their conversation, meanwhile, was driving northward at a sedate pace; she had no desire to attract the attention of a traffic cop. The car was the dark blue convertible coupe they had bought last October; Jerome's heart had been set on it, impractical as it was for a New York winter. Ruth Granger probably liked convertibles, Doris thought, without bitterness. How could she have cared so much about Ruth and Jerome a mere six months ago? Now, in April, the car was a delight. It looked and ran like new after the winter in storage. Doris had the top back, and a vagrant spring breeze ruffled her hair. Well out of city traffic she ripped off her felt hat and tossed it onto the seat beside her. She savored every aspect of freedom, driving alone, with no one following, no one watching, no one caring where she went. The city was difficult—the little start of recognition she had come to dread in strangers who passed her on the street, and then turned to stare or whisper or grin. Occasionally one followed her; she had been asked for autographs. Speaking to strangers was the hardest thing, buying stockings and pretending to ignore the gleam of recognition in the clerk's eyes, getting the car from the garage. Well, she'd done it once, now, and it would never be quite so hard again. Strange to realize, though, that this was what had seemed to her, two short weeks ago, the acme of human bliss, to be alone, to be free, to be legally innocent, to be safe. With a definite physical effort she pushed back the memory of those nights when she had lain awake thinking about the electric chair. Nothing remained now but Adriana. She let her mind push a little into the future. A small apartment in the city with Adriana and Miss Wright —poor girl, she must try to make up to her somehow, for all she had innocently suffered. No men—she couldn't endure that. Work of some sort, though it wouldn't be easy to find. She wouldn't be welcome at any sort of volunteer work for quite a while yet. About the only kind of job she could hope for would be one that would capitalize on her notoriety, and she didn't want that. Would there be money enough to start a small shop of her own? That way she could use a pseudonym without seeming to be trying to hide. Her maiden name would be good for a shop—Doris Fortune.

Would her mother be willing to let her go back to the city? Mother had been wonderful right straight through. It must, in many ways, have been worse for her and Aunt Fanny than for Doris herself. Their generation had been so much more sheltered than Doris's; what had happened to her would have killed a gentlewoman twenty-five years ago. But gratitude couldn't keep her living on in West-chester forever, a superannuated daughter of the house. She thought then of the other alternative, and a chill fin-ger of doubt touched her heart. What had she done? Did she really love the feeling of the noose around her neck so much that she had deliberately put it back now that Dick had removed it? It was not death she was risking any longer. In the old-fashioned phrase it was worse-than-death. Worse for her, and how much worse for all the others—mother and Aunt Fanny and Dick and Adriana even. Why hadn't she been content to let well enough alone? Could she even now call off Dr. Owen? No one knew where she had gone; mother and Aunt Fanny were superlatively decent about pretending that this was like any other April, when she might take her car and come and go as she chose.

She swung into the drive leading up to the dignified old colonial house that was so perfect a background for mother and Aunt Fanny, and noted the other cars with a slight sinking of the heart. Then she saw that one of them was Dick's coupe. The other was an old Buick sedan, and looked vaguely familiar too. Why of course, it was Clif-ford Meredith's. Doris frowned involuntarily at thought of her brother-in-law, and then stopped with a clash of gears and leapt from the car.

"He's brought Adriana," she thought, running across the lawn. She had never liked her husband's family, but this was a gesture of good will that touched her heart. She pealed the doorbell impatiently, too eager to stop and rummage in the purse for her keys.

"Is Adriana here, Martha?" she blurted out, as her mother's cook-general opened the door.

"Why, no, Miss Doris," Martha looked atonished and lugubrious at the same time, a feat that not many people could have performed.

"Oh." Doris wished she had taken a moment's time to enter with more dignity, for Jerome's older brother without Adriana was quite a different matter. Through the hallway she could see that the living room was occupied by a family conference so portentous that the five people engaged in it appeared to fill the big room. She took a long breath and stepped forward, and as she did Dick was on his feet to welcome her. Dick was swell; his dark face was haggard with the strain of the last few months, and yet his first thought was still to smooth things over for her. He had never once reproached her for the stupid lie that had brought this horror on them all. He looked at her and grinned, and she grinned back. The bond between them was so close they had little need of words. Every look they exchanged called up all the intimacies of a shared childhood, when the tall, dark little boy and the tiny, dark little girl, so strangely alike and yet so sharply different, had been inseparable in their games of pretending.

Mother sat erect at the tea table; her busy hands moved steadily and surely among the fragile cups, the delicate plates of wafers and thin sliced bread and butter. By the perfection of her manner as hostess Doris could recognize how deeply she was perturbed. Aunt Fanny was fluttering helplessly between the tea table and the guests.

"Hello, Clif," Doris said. "Hello, Jane. Awfully sweet

of you to come around and offer me the right hand of fellowship so soon." The casual note, she realized instantly, was all wrong. Worse, it was ghastly. Her brother and sister-in-law were evidently not going to let bygones be bygones. She repressed a desire to giggle at the inappropriateness of the phrase, applied to murder, but she was sure that the nervous twitching of the corners of her lips did not escape Clifford.

"Good afternoon, Doris," he said in a sepulchral tone. "You're looking remarkably well."

"Nothing like escaping the electric chair to set you up," she answered brightly, aghast at herself. Clifford Meredith always affected her this way.

He flushed angrily as he said: "I'm glad you're choosing to be flip, Doris. It makes what I've come to say much easier. For our part, not one of us would ever have mentioned Jerome's death to you again. It's over and done. We accept the verdict of the law. We have no reproaches for the way your defense was handled; we cherish no bitterness against you."

"That's swell," Doris said. "That's just the way I feel about you, too. Mother, I think I'd rather have a cocktail than tea right now."

"Why certainly, dear. But I'm not sure Martha knows how. Would a glass of sherry do?"

"I'll make it," Dick said grimly, retreating toward the kitchen.

"Anybody join me? Clif? Jane? Aunt Fanny?"

"I believe I will, dear," Aunt Fanny chirped. Aunt Fanny had never touched alcohol in her fifty-seven years, but neither Dick nor Doris nor their mother showed any sign of surprise.

"Thank you, no," Jane Meredith said icily. "I didn't know you drank, Miss Scott."

"I didn't use to," Aunt Fanny said vaguely.

"Perhaps we'd better get to business while your head is still clear, Doris," Clifford suggested. "The fact is, I have the papers here and Richard to witness that everything is proper and legal, and I think you'd better sign over the guardianship of Adriana right now."

"Sign over—Adriana!" Doris sounded in her own ears like the ingenue in a bad melodrama. "Why, Clifford, you're insane. I'm just about ready to take Adriana back."

"Doris, I hoped I shouldn't have to argue this," he said, rubbing his thick, slightly graying hair with a weary gesture. "You showed such good sense before that I thought you realized as well as the rest of us do that you're not fit to take care of Adriana."

"Oh, no," she shook her head. "Maybe I showed good sense before, but not that good. Of course I wanted her kept away from the trial and the reporters, and—and I can never be grateful enough to your mother—to mother Meredith—for protecting her now. But she's my baby, Clifford. I can't give her up."

"Has it occurred to you that you may have to?"

"No, it hasn't," Doris said with bravado, noting to herself, in a detached way, that it was a lie.

"I shouldn't have been so foolish as to come here to plead with you." Clifford went on. "You ought to realize, Doris, that if I ask you to do this voluntarily, it's only

because I hold some trump cards. Nevertheless I do ask
you. Mother adores Adriana. The baby is all that's left to
her of Jerome."

"She's all that's left to me of Jerome."

"I think you'll admit, Doris, that that's a little different."

"I don't see why. I didn't kill him. I've demonstrated
that to the satisfaction of the State of New York."

"The State of New York has given you the benefit of a
reasonable doubt, you mean. But I didn't come to reproach you. Personally I shouldn't care about Adriana, if
you want her. But I came here for mother's sake."

"Your mother hates me," Doris said. "She's always
hated me. She couldn't bear to give up Jerome to anyone—
her baby—and he was a grown man. Your mother's a
dreadful woman, and nothing in the world would make
me leave my baby with her."

"Steady, Doris," Dick said, coming back with the drink.

Doris took it with fingers that trembled.

"There's no more to be said." Clifford rose to his feet
and gestured to Jane. "We will start the necessary legal
action at once."

"You can't get Adriana by legal action—they can't, can
they, Dick?"

"We'll deal with them," he said grimly.

"You're making a great deal of unnecessary trouble and
grief for your sister if you persuade her to fight this, Mr.
Fortune," Clifford said. "There are numerous grounds on
which we can demonstrate that she is not a fit person to
have custody of a child. For one thing, she testified in

open court that she knew Jerome had relations with other women, but that she made no protest. What possible reason could there be for that except that she desired the same freedom for herself?"

"But that's outrageous," Doris gasped. "Twisting that—"

"You didn't mind blackening Jerome's character to save yourself. I don't suppose you even thought of the agony that evidence meant to mother."

"I think Jerome was the person to have thought of that."

"Stop squabbling, Doris." Mrs. Fortune's voice cut authoritatively through the babble. "It's obvious we're none of us in a mood to thresh this thing out today."

"There's nothing to thresh out," Clifford said. "Mother gets that baby, amicably or not. Think it over, Doris; if you'll see it our way we may be able to arrange for you to see her sometimes."

"I'll see you to the door," Aunt Fanny cut in brightly. "Martha's busy just now. Where *did* she put your hats?"

"In the hall closet, Fanny," mother said quietly.

"Can they do it, Dick?" Doris swallowed her drink in one gulp, and sat down on the sofa.

"We'll fight 'em all the way, Doris."

"Oh, Dick, I haven't any fight left."

"Then I'll fight it. As a matter of fact it might be a damn good idea to start a backfire. It strikes me the whole Meredith family was just a little too cocksure about how that murder happened for people who didn't know anything about it."

"Why, Dick, what do you mean?" It was Aunt Fanny,

speaking sharply and incisively. No one could ever tell how alcohol would affect people.

"I mean that if this mystery's ever to be solved, we've got to solve it. The police have washed their hands. They made an arrest, and as far as they're concerned, that's the end of it. But this business today makes it perfectly clear that an acquittal isn't the end of it for us. It'll haunt Doris all her life unless we can find out who really did it, and by God I'm going to."

"But Dick, you can't." Doris's voice trembled with earnestness. "There aren't any clues. The apartment's been cleaned and redecorated; everybody who knew anything about it has told his story a hundred times. There's nothing left to do."

"There's plenty left to do. The Merediths seem pretty damned sure the criminal was someone close to Jerome. Maybe they'll find out two sides of a family can play at that game. Do you really hate Mrs. Meredith, Doris, or was that just histrionics?"

"I don't know," she said wearily. "I suppose I was exaggerating. We never liked each other, but we were always civil. It's hard to know what you really think yourself under a surface like that. She's not a fit person to raise a child; I know that much, but it looks as if I should have thought of it sooner."

"Dick, Doris, this is sheer nonsense." Mother's voice was cool and steadying. "It's been clear from the very beginning to anyone with a grain of sense that Jerome Meredith was shot by a marauder."

"O.K. Then we'll find that marauder."

"Oh, no, Dick." Doris's voice was rising toward a shriek. "You can't put some poor bum with no one to defend him through that."

"It's something of a dilemma," he said. "Mother won't have it a Meredith; you won't have it a bum. How about Miss Wright? Nobody ever tried very hard to do anything about that mysterious sedative except prove that you had given it to her before you left for the theater. How do we know she didn't take it after committing the crime? It'd be a pretty feeble alibi, but if it was, it worked."

"Miss Wright mustn't be tormented any more. She'd never seen either of us before that week; besides, she's still with Adriana and I've gone through a lot already to keep the child from being disturbed."

"But, good God, all of you, there's a murderer loose!"

"There are a great many things worse in this world than a murderer loose," Aunt Fanny put in. Her voice was preternaturally grave. Doris looked at her and noted with some alarm that she was on the verge of tears. A first cocktail at fifty-seven was serious business. "I want you to let this thing alone, Richard," she said with dignity, rising to her feet. "Doris wants you to let it alone and so does your mother. I command you to let it alone." There was an astonishing undercurrent of ferocity in Aunt Fanny's tone.

"Don't you worry a bit, Aunt Fanny." Dick was all tender solicitude. "I'll handle this so that no one will be disturbed except the murderer."

"That's exactly what I'm afraid of," Aunt Fanny said, and did burst into tears.

By an odd but by no means incredible coincidence, Mr. Thomas Granger was using almost exactly the same words at almost exactly the same moment. The strangeness of the coincidence was lessened rather than increased by the fact that he was discussing the same subject, and that, in itself, was hardly coincidental at all, for the Meredith murder case was still the subject of widespread gossip throughout the city. Mr. and Mrs. Granger sat in a luxuriously appointed office several floors above one of the most splendid stores on Fifth Avenue.

"That's what I'm afraid of," Tom Granger said, leaning back in his swivel chair and puffing rather violently on his oversize cigar.

His wife, slim and elegant, the perfect smart young Long Island matron, exquisitely dressed for a day in town, risked creasing her lovely forehead with a frown.

"I don't know what you're talking about."

"The Meredith case," he said, "and its effect on us. I don't think we can get a divorce this year without starting it up again."

Ruth Granger sat very still in the slick leather chair and kept her eyes fastened on the vista of Fifth Avenue below.

"So you knew all the time," she said at last, quietly.

"My dear," he said, "I don't know exactly how dumb you had me figured to be, but whatever your estimate, it was a little high."

"I don't see why you're telling me now," she said, after another silence.

"I'm telling you now because I've taken all I'm going to take from you. Perhaps I shall divorce you this year, and perhaps I shan't. For the present, I've just finished closing your charge account here, and all the others as well. I've arranged to sell your car. I'll continue to furnish you food and a place to sleep, and that's all you get from me from now on."

"But that's fantastic."

"Maybe. Just the same, I've done it."

"It will be worse than divorce if the gossip columnists get hold of it."

"And where are the gossip columnists to get hold of it? Credit managers, I have reason to believe, are proverbially discreet. And in this case it will pay you to be discreet too."

"But I can divorce you for that."

"Not in this state. And unless I've overlooked a little nest-egg somewhere, or unless you had a second string to your bow besides Jerome Meredith, you'll have a tough time getting to Reno, my sweet. You're not the type for hitch-hiking."

"Tom, you can't do that. It's mediaeval."

"I see. I can keep you in furs and jewels and perfume so that you'll be attractive to your gigolos, and that's civilized. There's nothing degrading, to a woman like you, in being kept, but to tighten up on the purse strings and make you feel your dependence—that's the act of a cad."

"But, Tom, if you hate me like that, why did you lie to keep me out of the Meredith case?"

"Shut up," he snapped.

He stood up, a big man who carried his well-distributed weight easily. You would have guessed him to be an all-American of ten years back, and you wouldn't have been wrong. He ran his big hands lightly over the buttons and switches on his desk, checked the dictating machine, and walked quietly to the door. He swung it open with one quick gesture, and his secretary looked up in surprise from her desk across the reception room.

"Get that Jeffries letter right out, will you, Miss Adams? He wants confirmation." He shut the door and walked back to his swivel chair.

"That's a hell of a way to talk where you might be overheard. It's a hell of a way to talk anywhere. We spent the evening of last December 3rd together at home. That's on record."

She looked at him with a light of dawning comprehension on her face.

"You wanted that alibi," she said softly. "That's why you said it. And I thought it was because you cared what happened to me."

"Don't get hysterical," he answered coolly. "It wouldn't be too hard to open that case again. The D.A.'d just as soon as not have a conviction on the books before he writes it off."

"You know something about it," she whispered. "You were there."

His fingers ran over the switches again, half automatically. "If I shot him, I'll never swing for it," he said. "I'm not that sort. If I did it—and please, my love, recollect that this isn't a confession—I did it right. If I were ever to commit a murder, it would be a murder with a purpose, and that purpose wouldn't be to get myself bumped off in the next six months."

She laughed suddenly, hysterically.

"You're boasting," she said. "You're acting just like a little boy that won't take a dare. You don't know anything more about it than I do. You're bluffing."

"Perhaps," he smiled. "But if you hope to avoid future embarrassment, my dear, I should advise you not to try to use any of your charge accounts."

Chapter 3

"Now this is perfectly simple and easy, Mrs. Meredith," Dr. Owen said. "People have all sorts of romantic notions about hypnosis, but there's nothing to it at all. It's a trivial little experiment; it means no more than the talking you've been doing to me these last few months. How well it works depends altogether on you—well, at least very largely on you. I shall have to do my part as best I can. Your part is to relax, trust me, stop worrying. I think you're going to be an excellent subject."

"I hope so, but, frankly, doctor, I'd prefer scapolomine."

"Scapolomine wouldn't do any good at the level of consciousness on which your hallucination appears to be. Its effect is practically that of any anesthetic—sets you to babbling nonsense, with a good proportion of your secrets mixed in. If I had reason to believe you were consciously trying to conceal anything from me, I might use it. But as it is, there's no use."

"And the same with a lie detector?"

"Only more so. They're very crude, really. As a matter

of fact they're useful only with the lowest class of criminals, and even there the evidence they provide needs to be very carefully weighed. They're infernal machines in the hands of fools."

"It's nice to know you don't rank me in the very lowest class of criminals, doctor."

"Quite the contrary. Now I'll go on chatting as long as you like to make you feel completely at ease, but whenever you're ready we'll start."

"I'm ready now."

"I shall use your first name; your response comes more easily and naturally that way. Very well, Doris, when you're quite comfortable, lean back and close your eyes. Good chair, isn't it? Shoes pinch? Want to slip them off? Anything else uncomfortable? Hair pins? How about a cushion for the small of your back? All right now? Perfectly easy? Ready to drop off to sleep? Open your eyes, then, will you, Doris, and look at this glass ball. Just watch it. Don't strain. Don't think about it. Don't try to hurry. Just watch the ball while you go to sleep. You're going to sleep, Doris. Your eyes are heavy—but keep them open and watch the ball. You're very sleepy, Doris. The light is making you sleepy. Go to sleep, Doris. Go to sleep. You're so sleepy. You want to sleep—"

She responded amazingly. He had seldom had a better hypnotic subject. She watched the ball with unwinking eyes, and in an astonishingly few minutes the lids grew heavy and her head nodded. This was a moment at which Dr. Owen always felt a thrill of excitement he distrusted as specious.

"Svengali Owen," he mocked himself with one half of his mind, and then chided himself sharply for allowing his concentration to weaken at this most important point.

"You are sleeping, Doris," he repeated, hoping there was no change in his tone to indicate the wandering of his attention. "You are sleeping now. You are sleeping very comfortably. You will sleep until I tell you to waken. You are sleeping now, Doris."

The head had fallen back against the chair. The arms rested lightly, but utterly relaxed, on its arms. The blue-veined eyelids quivered ever so delicately over the veiled eyes. Every part of the slight body told of sleep as profound as that of an exhausted child. And looking at her Hillis Owen felt something as he supposed a mother must feel watching a sleeping child. This was what two months of the woman had done to him. Insane! She was a witch, and five hundred years ago would have been burned at the stake as surely as she now sat sleeping in his office. He was plainly bewitched, and it was his duty to report the phenomenon at the next annual meeting of the psychiatric association.

It would be as sensible a report as any he could make on her. Twice a week since April he had listened to her talk about herself, her husband, her child, her brother, her parents and her aunt Fanny, her sex-life, forgotten memories of her childhood, the troubled fantasies of her adolescence, the delicate adjustments of her marriage, her dislike of her in-laws, her grief over her husband's unfaithfulness. He knew how much her father's suicide in 1929 had shadowed her girlhood. He knew more about her

now than her mother, her brother and her husband together or singly. He had a complete picture of her personality, and it was a thoroughly normal, wholesome and
well-integrated one. That is, if a psychiatrist could be
trusted to recognize a normal personality when he encountered one. It was definitely a novelty in his profession.
He had found so little that he was ashamed to send her a
bill. A well-to-do woman, they said, always got her
money's worth from a course of psychoanalysis, particularly when the analyst was a young and handsome man.
As far as that went, sex didn't need to enter into it at all.
Anyone liked talking about himself at length to an interested listener. Even if all its practitioners were utter idiots,
psychoanalysis was still a boon to mankind. Dr. Owen
grinned at himself for sitting still rationalizing his own
profession instead of getting on with the business in hand.

His opinion of the value of hypnosis was not very high.
It was useful sometimes as a means of conveying sugges-
tions to a stubborn neurotic, but he had never before used
it, as he was using it today, to find out something that
psychoanalysis had failed to turn up. He was quite certain
that Doris Meredith was concealing nothing from him.
She had shown him the whole of a remarkably well-bal-
anced personality. Her emotional conflicts were pretty
well resolved; she had no bad repressions. He might well,
he thought, recommend being defendant in a murder
trial to several of his more badly inhibited patients. It was
a rather heroic method, of course, but it did seem to
throw light into the hidden recesses of the mind. Mrs.
Meredith chatted glibly the semi-scientific jargon of the

reasonably well-read woman of her generation. She worried over whether her simple, animal love for Adriana was a "mother fixation," and whether an occasional reluctance to adapt herself to her husband's convenience could have been legitimately described as frigidity.

That she was thoroughly sane and essentially sound Hillis had no doubt whatsoever. But as to whether or not she had killed her husband he remained miserably undecided. In April he would have said that it was an impossible crime for a woman such as he now knew her to be. But he had learned a good deal since April. Human nature is a strange and humbling study. Meanwhile Mrs. Meredith sat sleeping in his subject's chair, waiting for him to begin. And Dr. Owen knew with perfect clarity that he was fiddling away the time in meditation because he didn't want to start. That was the great disadvantage of being a psychiatrist; it made it so hard to fool yourself.

"It is the night of December 3rd, Doris," he said, in the same tone of voice he had been using when he left off speaking. "You have been at the theater with Dick. It's the first intermission. You are going home. You're riding in a taxicab. You're thinking about what you are going to do when you get home. The taxi is drawing up at your door. You have the money in your hand. You're ready to hurry into the building."

He felt a slight prickling of his scalp as she sat forward in the chair, leaning on her right arm, her hand closed as if it held several loose small coins. Now he was for it! No turning back!

"The taxi has stopped now, Doris. You're paying the

driver. You're hurrying into the building."

The pantomime was abrupt and frightening. She stood up and backed away from the chair; holding her closed hand out abruptly toward the chair she had just quitted, she turned it over suddenly and opened it. Dr. Owen could almost hear the jingling of coins. Here was a Trilby worth his efforts. With her left hand she gathered up the skirt of her sharkskin suit, as if to keep a trailing velvet skirt well above the sidewalk. She ran trippingly, on the toes of her stockinged feet, broke her pace to push against a heavy door, and then ran again. She pulled up short at the elevator, and pushed the bell impatiently, hard and long. She hadn't told him that, Hillis noted. He had assumed that she'd found the automatic elevator on the main floor. How long had she had to wait, and who had been using the elevator? Had any notice of it been taken at the trial? Would the thing never come? She pushed again on the button in thin air, long and hard, and the look of strain and despair on her face brought out a fine perspiration on Hillis Owen's forehead. Then she pushed back the door, fast and hard, stepped in and waited a moment for the door to shut while she reached up tentatively for the button that would take her to her floor. She pushed it. Six, Dr. Owen remembered. The button was just about the height of her eyes. She waited, skirt gathered in her hand, small, shoeless toe tapping faintly in impatience. There was a slight, intent frown between her eyes. She stepped forward, out of the elevator, and turned to the left, fumbling in an imaginary bag for an imaginary key. The gesture was vague and helpless. Should he have given her something to hold? She had it. She was fitting it into a door. The lock caught for a moment—now it gave. She was pushing the door open, and now, suddenly, she was moving with caution and as quietly as a panther. Dr. Owen clenched his teeth to keep from saying the word that would break the spell. She walked silently down the hall on the toes of her stockinged feet. She turned to the right. "The kitchen and a dropped living room are to the right" she had said. Perhaps she had no sense of direction. She was going down two steps. The pantomime was unmistakable. Dr. Owen cursed himself for a fool, silently and bitterly. He *would* regard this with scientific detachment. Deliberately he unclenched his hands, and noted the depressions where the nails had bit into the palms. Doris Meredith was standing perfectly still and laughing.

"I've just left one comedy melodrama," she said, "and I walk into another."

Not very good, but then, no doubt she was upset. How was it she had told him? "I laughed and said something about melodrama."

She turned around squarely and faced the doctor. Her eyes were wide open, clear and angry. She walked stiffly back up the two imaginary stairs, across the foyer and into another room—the bedroom she shared with her husband, of course. She looked, for a moment, into an imaginary mirror, and then opened a drawer and rummaged in it. When she turned around again her empty right hand was weighed down as if by a heavy metal object.

"Stop her, stop her, stop her, stop her, stop her, don't let her do it again," something was saying monotonously over and over again in the back of Dr. Owen's mind. Nice work, playing Svengali. Lots of fun to hold the mirror up to nature.

Doris walked steadily back the way she had come, stepped down the two steps, lifted the heavy right hand steadily to shoulder height. When it was fully extended, she pulled back with her index finger, and stood for a moment staring. Her arm dropped to her side. She turned again and walked, a little unsteadily, up those two eternal steps, across the foyer, and into another door. She leaned across a crib, her face tender, her left arm shielding the child's eyes from the light, her right, still clinging to the heavy object, dropped at her side. She walked out of that room and into another, and pantomimed wiping the gun clean with a towel. Then she went back to the inevitable steps, but this time she hesitated, and instead of going down into the room, leaned over and dropped a gun. She'd have made a damned good actress, the doctor thought. You could almost hear the thud as it fell. Then she turned a last time, and hurried out without looking back. She rode down in the elevator, went to the door, gave a little start of surprise, and then, after a moment's hesitation, stepped into the taxi. She leaned back again in her chair, her face tired, her breathing heavy. She was worn out. And no wonder, he thought. So that was how it happened. And now he would have to wake her and tell her. Damn it, what was wrong? Where was the detail in the perfect panto-mime that seemed false? It was there somewhere? Could he make her do it again? Cruel, she was exhausted already. This would lay her up for a week. He could postpone tell-

ing her, but even then he'd made her live all through it
again.

"You're in a taxi," he said quietly, his voice showing no
hint of the strain under which he labored. "It is the evening of December 3rd. You have been at a theater with
your brother. It's the first intermission. You are going
home. You're thinking about what you are going to do
when you get there. The cab is drawing up at your door.
You have the money in your hand. You're ready to hurry
into the building."

He was a brute to do it. There was no sense to it. Only
—if he could settle the thing once and for all—now. Where
was the tiny nagging discrepancy?

Her weary face was eager again; she was sitting forward
in the chair in the attitude of tense expectancy. The cab
stopped and she went through it again—paying, hurrying
into the house, waiting for the elevator, getting out and
fishing for her key, working with it a moment before she
could push the door open. Now again she was tiptoeing
stealthily across a foyer—straight across it. Wasn't that
the place where she should have swerved to the right?
She tiptoed ahead, her face turned toward the left. She
turned to the left, and after a moment silently pushed open
a door. She made a gesture of switching on an electric light
with infinite caution. She crossed to a crib, and stood looking down in the same position as before, her face tender
and vulnerable. Then she looked across her shoulder with
a frown. Her husband? No, she wasn't looking high enough
to be facing a man standing erect. The sleeping nursemaid,
of course. On a cot in the nursery, no doubt. She tiptoed

across the room and reached one hand out, tentatively, and then drew it back. Still frowning, she looked about the room, noting, no doubt, the raised window, the orderly array of toys and clothes, and again the sleeping baby. She reached the hand out again, and this time it touched a breathing body. She did not shake the shoulder she held, however, but after a moment shrugged and turned back to the crib. She leaned over and touched the sleeping child with her lips, turned out the light, and went noiselessly out of the room. Again she tiptoed delicately across the foyer. She did not turn her face toward the room down into which two steps led, but went directly to the entrance door and let herself out.

Hillis watched the remaining pantomime in bewilderment. What did it mean? Had she gone back a second time? Was she acting through all of this? Could she be tricking him? Was her hallucination so deeply planted in her mind that even in hypnotism she could not be released? Worse, how had he varied the key words so as to set her off one way the first time and another the second? The answer to the whole riddle very probably lay right there, and he didn't know. He ran frantically over his words, but he could remember no variation. Doris was back in her chair, resting, utterly relaxed again, the lines of exhaustion easing on her face. In a minute he would have to wake her and tell her—what? That her problem was exactly what it had been when she came to him. Of course he could wrap it up nicely in the jargon of his profession, except that he still didn't know whether it was defense mechanism or suggestion. Tell her not to worry; tell her she was well-integrated. What was wrong with the murder pantomime?

"All right, Doris," he said. "You've finished. You can wake up now. You're waking. You are awake."

She opened her eyes and looked at him without raising her head.

"Tired?" he asked brightly. "Rest for awhile. You did splendidly. An excellent subject."

She didn't ask about the outcome of the experiment. She looked at him quietly for some seconds, and then said, with a faint smile:

"Somebody—Poe, I think—wrote a story about mesmerism when it was new. A dying man was mesmerized, and the process of death was arrested for some weeks. But when he was awakened the corpse fell instantly into a mass of rotten corruption."

"The Facts in the Case of M. Valdemar," he said.

"I feel like that." She laughed and raised one hand waveringly to her forehead.

"Yes," he said. "It's a hard day's work." He deliberately ignored the pleading in her eyes.

"I suppose the news is bad," she had to say at last, "or you'd have told me at once."

"Not bad, just inconclusive. The experiment wasn't a success. I tried to warn you that it might not be."

"Didn't I respond?" Her eyes widened. "What have I been doing to wear me out so?"

"Oh, yes, you responded." He laughed grimly. "You responded altogether too well. You've been acting all over the place—*both* versions of what you did at your

apartment on the evening of December 3rd." He hadn't
intended to tell her. There was something about her that
played hob with all his professional discretion. "You
haven't by any chance been deliberately playing a little
comedy for me?" he asked.

"Not that I know of," she answered humbly. She
wasn't even angry at him. She hadn't a word of blame for
her wasted time and money.

"I'm afraid I made a great mistake in accepting you
as a patient, Mrs. Meredith," he said abruptly, more
formally than he had spoken to her for some weeks, to
cover his own embarrassment. "To tell you the truth, you
don't need a doctor. You need a detective. I don't think
you shot your husband, but I can't speak with certainty,
and I don't see how anyone can unless the true culprit is
found and convicted. You must have sensed, I think, that
my own opinion has changed in the course of my psychiatric investigation. I find you a sound personality. That
doesn't absolutely rule out the possibility that you committed murder, of course. Sane, well-integrated people do
that, but when they do it's usually under intolerable provo-
cation, and it doesn't sound to me as if any of your dif-
ferences with your husband deserved to be so described.
However, the borderline between thought and action is
admittedly a province where psychiatrists are at a loss.
We understand pretty well how thought processes are
carried on, the mechanics of suppression and so on, but
the point at which thought passes over into action, and
why it varies so widely in different individuals, is all *terra
incognita* to us. Pardon my Latin, please; it's a trick we

doctors have when we don't want to be forced to say 'I don't know' in plain English. I think I've done everything I can for you. You are certainly sane; as I told you two months ago, there is every reason to believe that your memory will eventually adjust itself on this painful matter, and you need have no fear for the future, as to whether you're a responsible mother for your child, I mean, or about remarriage. If I were in your position and had this thing nagging at me, I'd hire a good private detective and have it sifted to the bottom."

"That's what my brother wants to do," she said, "but I can't bear to run the risk of putting some other innocent person—some innocent person—through the torture I've just undergone."

"That's your decision," he said. "I'm afraid I've gone as far as I can."

"You mean you're dismissing me?"

"My dear lady, I'm afraid I've done everything I can for you."

She sat looking at him steadily, and her eyes filled with tears like those of a little girl.

"Oh, Mrs. Meredith, Doris, don't."

"Surely you've seen patients cry before." She wiped away the tears, laughing a little at his rueful face. "I should think it would be a very usual part of your routine."

"Perhaps, but it still distresses me." He wouldn't say: "Perhaps it's because you are a very special sort of a patient."

"I wish I were a detective," he went on, partly to keep her mind off the tears. "You know there was something in that first pantomime not quite right—the first time you killed him; the second you just looked at the baby—and I still can't place it. As a matter of fact, that's the reason I had you try it again. I don't know whether you left out something or did something wrong or put in something that didn't belong, but somehow it wasn't quite true. Whatever it was, it added to the strength of my belief that you didn't commit the crime. And then when I tried to get you to act it out again, you did the other thing."

"I still dream it," she said. "Perhaps I can supply you the detail from the dream some time. Something that rings just a little false?"

"Forget it," he advised. "Forget the whole business. If you don't want to hire a detective, take up golf or gardening. Get your mind off this."

"I'll try, doctor," she said. She hesitated, and then went on. "I've never told you, because it's a recent development and has no connection with what you've been trying to do for me, but I'm having some trouble getting Adriana back. My mother-in-law has her. She took her originally for the duration of the trial. Of course at the time I wasn't thinking any too clearly, nor planning very far ahead. I was grateful for her kindness. But now the whole Meredith family is very bitter toward me, and they're taking legal action to keep her away from me. This happened just after I first came to you. I shouldn't want them to know I had been your patient; even though you can give me a clean bill of health, the fact that I've consulted a psychiatrist might give them a handle against me. I hope your professional responsibility will allow you to keep it secret that I have been your patient."

"Certainly. You still haven't told anyone of your fear?"

"Not even my brother."

"I dare say you're right; if it got about it could start gossip that would hurt you. I'm sorry about the child. If anything I could do would help—"

"Thank you. If I ever need your testimony about my wholesome personality I'll call on you. And for the present, good-bye, and thank you."

She stood up and held out her hand with a gesture completely friendly and confiding. He pressed it with professional warmth, and followed her to the door. It was late; dusk had fallen and the waiting room was empty. Dr. Owen had intentionally kept the afternoon free for his experiment. Miss Pomeroy looked up brightly from her desk.

"Good-bye, Miss Pomeroy," Doris said. "I'm discharged. Good-bye, doctor."

"Good-bye, Mrs. Meredith. Good luck. It's been a pleasure to know you."

"And you, too, both of you."

She stepped out into the corridor and walked away, a gallant little figure against the gathering gloom. Dr. Owen let the door swing to, and turned to face the accusing glare of his office nurse.

Miss Pomeroy said nothing. She looked hard at the doctor, and then returned to her typing. Dr. Owen moodily scuffed the rug, and walked back and forth across the room.

"What else could I do, Pomeroy?" he burst out at last, defensively.

Miss Pomeroy went on typing until he sat on the edge of her desk and put his big hand over the keys.

"Stop it, Pomeroy. I need consolation. I failed that dame, but I don't see what else I could have done. Would you have wanted me to tell her I was sure she didn't do it when I'm not? Haven't you any professional ethics?"

Miss Pomeroy took off her glasses and sat back in her chair.

"She didn't respond to hypnosis, then?"

"She responded too damned well—beg pardon, Pomeroy. She acted it all out both ways. She did and she didn't. We're right back where we started from."

"But you don't believe now that she did it, do you, doctor?"

"Touché. No, I don't. And in April I did. I told her that, for what consolation it may be to her. She's a game kid. She got under my skin."

"I like her too," Miss Pomeroy said. "What will she do now?"

"I advised her to hire a detective, but I don't think she will. She's afraid of picking up somebody innocent and putting 'em through the mill. Besides, she says it's too late. The clues are all gone. Damn it, if I was a detective, I'll bet I could turn one up."

Miss Pomeroy looked hard at him until he flushed and laughed.

"Not so hot at my own job, but I could sure do the other fellow's."

"Well, why don't you?" Miss Pomeroy asked.

"Why don't I what?"

"Investigate it yourself. There's no law against prying as long as you don't take a fee for it."

Dr. Owen stared at his precise, ethical, and respectable nurse as if she had suddenly said: "Heil Hitler."

"Why, Pomeroy, you're crazy," he said gently. "This job has gone to your head. Take a vacation. Take a rest cure. How long have you been feeling odd? Why didn't you tell me?"

"My favorite recreation is reading detective stories, Doctor Owen," she said. "I am sure I would be a much better investigator than nine-tenths of those who are held up as examples of splendid practitioners of the art of detecting. Most of them simply wait until all the suspects have been killed except one, and arrest that one. You could certainly do better than that."

"Why, Pomeroy," he said, "I do believe you mean it seriously. Detective stories are all very well, but this is life. Take this concrete case for example. If you wanted to find out the truth about who murdered Jerome Meredith, where would you start? I wouldn't have the foggiest notion."

"I would," she said. "I'd talk to Mrs. Granger. She knows at the very least whether or not Mrs. Meredith shot him, and I think I could make her talk."

"I'll bet you could," he said reverently. "Pomeroy, you tempt me. But how about my profession? I have patients to see."

"Finding out who killed Mrs. Meredith's husband

wouldn't take up any more of your time than chess does now."

"Quick, Watson, the needle." Dr. Owen leaned back on her desk, his hands clasped about one knee, his eyes sparkling with the pleasure of the notion. "But no, Pomeroy, you'd never do for Watson. You're much too quick. You'd show me up the first time I tried a deduction."

"My mother intended to name me Watson if I had been a boy," Miss Pomeroy said sedately.

He smacked the desk hard.

"That does it. It's fate. We're in it, Pomeroy. I'm game if you are."

He picked up her telephone quickly, before he should have time to change his mind.

"If you're trying to call Mrs. Meredith, she'll hardly have had time to reach her room."

"She's staying at the Shelton. She could just about have made it.—Mrs. Jerome Meredith, please. Ring again, will you; she should be just coming in. Very well, then, ask her to call Dr. Owen at Plaza 9-7300, will you?"

He put down the instrument. "I'm going to take her out to dinner and talk it all over on a strictly non-psychiatric basis. Come along, Pomeroy?"

"Two's company; three's a crowd. But I'll be glad to call on Mrs. Granger."

"Better wait until I get you the green light on that. We don't want to be officious, after all."

The phone rang, and he picked it up eagerly.

"Hello, Doris? Yes, this is Hillis Owen. Not Doctor this time. Are you busy this evening? Could you have dinner with me somewhere? I'd like to talk this all over un-professionally."

She hesitated, obviously startled, and he suddenly felt ridiculous. It was not a sensation to which he was accustomed, and he didn't like it.

"This is awfully abrupt and awkward," he said. "Miss Pomeroy's been giving me a talking to. I feel that I've failed you as a doctor. And I'd really like to go on from where we left off, as a friend."

"I couldn't think of troubling you further, Dr. Owen," she said coldly.

"Doris, I'm sorry. I'm saying this very badly. I want very much to talk with you. Won't you have dinner with me, please? As a favor? Then if you want to squelch me, I'll squelch gracefully."

Three hours later, sitting opposite her in the air-conditioned comfort of a small restaurant in the East Fifties, he felt more ridiculous than ever. She had changed to a street length dress of some thin black stuff with a jewelled clip at her breast. Her dark hair was swept up and piled on top of her head, giving her an added dignity. Her poise, as always, was perfect. She had, he reflected bitterly, one of the best lawyers in New York for a twin brother. And here was he, Hillis Owen, a good man in his own field, going out of his way to stick an inexpert finger into a scandalous pie.

When Doris finally understood what he was offering to do—and no wonder it baffled her; it struck him now as a notion unequalled for effrontery and ignorance—she was as graciously tactful as if he had been a bungling high school boy.

"I can't refuse such kindness, of course," she said, "and it reassures me that you do think I'm innocent. But how could we start? What could you do?"

He thought it better to omit Miss Pomeroy's suggestion at the moment.

"You could introduce me to your brother," he said, "just as a personal friend, of course. Tell him I'm interested in sleuthing in an amateur way, and ask him to let me work on it with him. He never did hire a detective?"

"No," she said, "and he still doesn't know I've been consulting a psychiatrist."

"That's all right. I'd just as soon leave my professional reputation out of this anyway. Introduce me as Dr. Owen, of course—after all, we don't want any hole-and-corner business, but leave the implication that our acquaintance is purely social."

"All right. But Dick may cross-question you."

"I think I can stand up to it."

"I have the keys for the 52nd Street apartment," she said slowly. "I don't suppose there's anything there. I've never been able to bear the thought of going back myself. First the police were all through it, and later Dick arranged to have it cleaned and the personal things moved. He thought there was no point in trying to sublet; said we'd just have a bunch of sensation hunters tramping through it. Our lease runs until October. Would you want to take the keys and see if you can find anything there? Of course it's most unlikely."

"It might throw some light on what was wrong with that reconstruction of yours," he said. "Yes, give me the keys. And just as part of the camouflage for your brother, don't you think we'd better both use first names?"

"I can't see why you're doing this, Hillis," she answered. He snuffed out his cigarette with a savage gesture.

"I wish I couldn't," he said.

Chapter 4

DURING the ensuing week Miss Grace Pomeroy made for the first time the astonishing discovery that life does not follow the pattern of detective novels. When Dr. Owen told her that Mrs. Meredith had agreed they might go ahead, she set to work at once on the problem of how to approach Mrs. Granger. After considering it in all her spare moments for a full day, she was obliged to admit to herself that it appeared to be completely impossible. In a detective novel she would have been a close friend of the Chief Inspector or the District Attorney, and could have gone directly to the home of anyone she wanted to interview and interviewed him or her thoroughly and with dispatch. But this was real life, and all she knew about Mrs. Thomas Granger was what she had read in the newspaper, and what she had heard, in the inviolable sanctuary of a doctor's consulting room, from Mrs. Meredith. If it were even a problem in which Dr. Owen could have concerned

himself officially, things would have been much simpler.
It might have been possible to go to a complete stranger
on a matter concerning a patient of Dr. Hillis Owen. But
for Miss Grace Pomeroy, nurse, to go to Long Island and
ask impertinent questions of Mrs. Thomas Granger, social-
ite, because her name had been mentioned in a murder
trial, was so plainly impossible that even Miss Pomeroy's
invincible optimism was forced to bow to facts.

She said nothing to Dr. Owen, but set herself grimly
to find a way. It would be too bitter to be balked at the
very threshold of her first murder investigation. It was undeniably awkward to be in the position of an inquisitive
bystander. She inquired cautiously among her acquaintances for a line in the direction of Mrs. Granger; she turned
over in her mind the desperate expedient of writing Mrs.
Granger a letter introducing herself and asking for an
interview. But she had absolutely nothing to offer in return. A busy week had passed without any further reference, between doctor and nurse, to the murder investigation, when Dr. Owen asked one day:

"How are you coming with Mrs. Granger, Pomeroy?"

"Well, to tell you the truth, doctor, I haven't been able
to think of a way to get to see her. Do you suppose I could
disguise myself as a reporter?"

"No, I don't," he said gravely, "but I've got a better
scheme." He handed her a note. "Read that."

It was on a heavy sheet of cream-colored linen. The
writing was in the fashionable bold, angular feminine
script.

Dear Doris:

I've never written or called to congratulate you on
your acquittal. It's a point Emily Post doesn't cover very
thoroughly. But you've known all along how happy I am
for you, haven't you, darling? Now that I am writing, I'm
afraid I'll have to be rather crass. The fact is, I need money
so badly that I'm willing to tell you something which I
think should be worth paying for. Will you come out and
see me as soon as you can? In the daytime if, as I suppose,
you'd prefer not to run into Tom. I haven't a car at my disposal just now or perhaps I could come to you. Let me
know ahead of time.

Affectionately, Ruth.

Miss Pomeroy read it three times. The first time she
was not so much interested in the implications of the
note as in the proof that there was, after all, a god in the
machine, and he was working for her. She wanted to see
Mrs. Granger and she was going to see Mrs. Granger. She
smiled with satisfaction and read the letter again. That
time and the next she read it more slowly, and the smile
changed to a frown.

"Blackmail?" she asked finally.

"I hardly think so," he said. "If that's what she has in
mind, this letter is evidence. Blackmail's a crime, and Mrs.
Granger is a smart enough woman to know it. I think she
means she has some information to sell. The reason is
beyond me. Doris says the Grangers have money to burn."

"Maybe she's been burning too much of it," Miss
Pomeroy commented grimly.

"Well, do you want to see her?"

"Of course I do."

"Doris doesn't. She's written out an authorization for you to represent her. It's nothing official. She thought her brother would scare Mrs. Granger into keeping her mouth shut, whereas you, Pomeroy, can be as wise as a serpent and as gentle as a dove."

He handed her a note-size calling card with a message scrawled on it.

Dear Ruth: Miss Pomeroy is a good and confidential friend of mine. I don't feel up to talking about Jerome's murder myself, but you can talk very freely to her and depend on her answers. Hastily, Doris.

"That ought to put her in her place," Miss Pomeroy said. "She won't like me very well to start off with."

"Are you game to tackle her anyway?"

"Nothing could stop me."

"Well, there's nothing pressing here this afternoon. Go ahead. Take a day off. And Pomeroy, for gosh sakes, call me the minute you get back to town."

Riding out to Long Island on a nearly empty noon train, Miss Pomeroy planned her approach. She was frankly nervous. People as rich as the Grangers patronized Dr. Owen professionally of course. In her capacity as nurse she had been in houses like theirs. But this time she was not going as a nurse.

The taxi driver at the station to whom she gave the address evinced no surprise. He grunted acquiescence and started off with a jerk. Miss Pomeroy sat stiffly upright on

the seat and clutched her purse, watching the shifting landscape. The taxi swung off the main highway on to a
gravelled country road, and again onto a lane before they
reached Gray Rocks, the Granger's place. "Place" would
be what they would call it, Miss Pomeroy was certain. It
was a little small for an estate, but definitely too imposing
for a farm. The house was gray, like the name, and mildly
gothic. Miss Pomeroy didn't know much about architecture, but she knew it was bastard. She sniffed when she saw
it, and felt more self-possessed.

The butler who let her in was friendly.

"Mrs. Granger is in the library, ma'am," he said. "This
way, if you please."

"You'd better take her this note first," Miss Pomeroy
said. "She doesn't know me."

"I'm sure she'll see you, ma'am," the butler answered
with a faint smile that caused Miss Pomeroy to close her
mouth without having asked why he should be sure.

Mrs. Granger was in the library, smoking and playing
solitaire, her feet curled beneath her in an easy chair. She
looked up eagerly as Miss Pomeroy followed the butler in,
and then frowned slightly, but rather in disappointment
than anger, Miss Pomeroy thought.

"Miss Grace Pomeroy" the butler said oracularly. "She
has a letter for you, Mrs. Granger." He bowed himself out
and left Miss Pomeroy face to face with the first adventure
of her detective career. Mrs. Granger was a tall, slender,
fair young woman with bright eyes and fingernails. She
looked like any number of the smart, chattering denizens

of the best cocktail bars.

"I have a note from Mrs. Meredith," Miss Pomeroy said in brisk, official tones, and handed it over.

Mrs. Granger glanced through it hastily.

"Couldn't face me, eh? I don't know that I blame her. Did you know Jerome Meredith, Miss Pomeroy? Must I call you that? Do you mind first names right off the bat?"

"Yes, I do," Miss Pomeroy said, answering the last question first. "I believe you must if you call me anything. No, I didn't know him."

Mrs. Granger looked startled and glanced at the note again. But the question of her caller's sponsorship seemed to bother her very little. It would have been perfectly simple to get in with a forged note, or with none at all.

"He wasn't the man for Doris," Ruth Granger was saying. "She's much too slow for him. Jerome would have been a perfectly good husband for a girl with a little more oomph. He got bored easily." She smiled reminiscently. Miss Pomeroy frowned.

"You'd like me to get to business, wouldn't you?" Mrs. Granger said. "Tea? Cigarette? Drink?"

"No, thank you. You said you had some information for Mrs. Meredith, Mrs. Granger. If you could tell me about it, I'd see that it got to her."

"Just who are you anyway? From her brother's office?"

"No, I'm not acquainted with Mr. Fortune. I'm acting as a personal friend."

"Doris doesn't seem very particular about what gossip gets around."

"I don't believe she thinks it matters now that the trial is over."

Ruth Granger lit another cigarette for herself and stood up.

"Of course I could say that I won't talk to a stranger, and that if Doris Meredith wants what I know she'll have to come to me to buy it. But, damn it, I'm in a hurry for my money, and if Doris doesn't care who I talk to I don't see why I should. All right then; here's my proposition. For one thousand dollars cash I'll tell Doris or you or any-one else she chooses to send everything I know about Jerome Meredith's murder, and I'll promise not to tell any-one else."

"Frankly I can't see the point of that," Miss Pomeroy said. "Mrs. Meredith has nothing whatever to gain, and you, it seems to me, have a good deal to lose."

"To lose?"

"You testified at the trial, and if what you said then wasn't true, you've committed perjury, haven't you? And if this is something Mrs. Meredith wants you to keep secret, what guarantee could you give her beyond your promise?"

"Look, Miss Pomeroy." The younger woman's voice was suddenly savage. "I need a thousand dollars very badly. I'll put my cards on the table. I want a divorce. I can't get one here. I'll have to get to Reno. My husband has cut off all my money. I haven't a cent but what I can cadge from the servants. Even the household bills go through the housekeeper's hands, not mine. I haven't a car; I haven't money for a railroad ticket to town or a matinee, or even a movie out here. I can't pay my bridge losses. You can't conceive of what it's like. I had to get the stamp for my letter to Doris from the butler. The servants are quite decent about little amounts; they must have been getting away with a good deal themselves to be so sympathetic. Tom would like to see me not able to write a letter. I have my food here, and a place to sleep, and what clothes I had on hand, and that's all. It's horrible."

"I'm very sorry, Mrs. Granger. But isn't there some legal redress? Surely your husband could be compelled to make you an allowance."

"I don't know. All the lawyers I know except Doris's brother are Tom's. I've written one, but he says as long as Tom is keeping me I have no kick coming. If I can get to Reno, though, I can get a divorce and alimony. I've figured I can do it on a thousand, pay the lawyer and live the six weeks out there. But I must have a thousand."

"Can't you borrow it?"

"No luck so far."

"But, Mrs. Granger—excuse me if I seem impertinent, but if I understand correctly, you're planning to dabble in crime in order to get this money. Wouldn't it be much wiser and safer to put up with this for a while? Your husband will come round in time."

"My husband knows I loved Jerome Meredith, and he'll never come round."

"Oh, well then, I don't know what to say. Mrs. Meredith didn't empower me to offer any money, and I'm almost sure she wouldn't have anything like a thousand dollars. It's a lot of money, Mrs. Granger. Perhaps it doesn't seem so much to you, but to most people it's a fortune. Couldn't you sell your jewelry?"

"It's all in the safe deposit vault, and Tom has the key. I suppose I could steal a few little trinkets around the house and pawn them, but I should feel such a fool. Same way with borrowing. And I really have something for Doris."

"I scarcely know what to say."

"Tell her this. I was at the Meredith apartment on the night of December 3rd. I went by appointment. But I didn't get in. I—perhaps she knows I had a key. But it wouldn't work that night. The door was bolted from inside, and I couldn't get in."

Mrs. Granger stopped and looked straight at Miss Pomeroy, who was sitting on the edge of her chair.

"Tell her that," she said. "If she wants to know what I heard, she can pay me the thousand."

Miss Pomeroy sat back as if a dash of cold water had been flung into her face. Her brain raced, trying to fit together the pieces of the puzzle.

"You were at the door of the Meredith apartment on the evening of December 3rd. You didn't get inside, but you heard something. What time was that?"

"Have you ever listened to a side-show barker, Miss Pomeroy? Do it some time; it's instructive. That's the technique I'm using now; I've told all I'm going to tell until I get a thousand dollars."

"I don't know exactly how far I'm authorized to go for Mrs. Meredith. But it's only fair to tell you that I don't think you'll get that money. If I were in your position, Mrs. Granger, I'd try to find a job."

"What could I use for a commutation ticket? I have no decent clothes. And besides, I don't know how to do anything that anybody pays money for."

"I'm not quite sure," Miss Pomeroy went on slowly, "whether you're offering to tell Mrs. Meredith something you think she will want to know, or to keep quiet about something that you think she doesn't want known."

Mrs. Granger laughed. "That's all right. She'll know."

Somehow Miss Pomeroy felt that she was not managing this interview very well. Quite definitely Mrs. Granger appeared to be keeping the upper hand. She tried to remember how you started in pumping people. Mrs. Granger was as disconcertingly frank in some respects as she was determinedly uncommunicative in others.

"Perhaps she'll know," she conceded, "but still it makes quite a difference in the situation. If you are offering her information that she can use in solving the mystery of her husband's murder you'll have to be willing to stand by your testimony if it's to be of any use. On the other hand, if you're suggesting blackmail—which would seem a foolish thing to do through an intermediary—she'd be a fool to pay you without getting some assurance that you were really going to keep quiet."

"So you want me to tell you which is my game." Mrs. Granger laughed. "Well, I won't do it. As the kids say, that's for me to know and you to find out. I'll tell you this much, though. My testimony's on record in a court of law. I don't want to be arrested for perjury. Officially I stand on what I've said. If Doris is curious enough to know what I really heard, she can pay me a thousand dollars. And I'm willing to bet that she is."

"Suppose I go straight to the police with this story?"

"I'd deny it. No, I wouldn't. They could find out you were really here, and about Tom and the money. Wait a minute. I'd say that I was there at the door that night, but I didn't hear anything; that I needed the money so badly I was gambling on Doris's knowing something about it and getting scared."

"But that would be admitting perjury and extortion too."

"But you're not going to the police."

"No," Miss Pomeroy confessed sadly. "I suppose I'm not." She stood up. "There's really nothing more to say, is there? I'll give Mrs. Meredith your message. You could have written it just as well, you know, and saved me the trip out here."

"And missed meeting you? But how dreadful! I haven't much to amuse me these days."

Miss Pomeroy resolved on a Parthian shot in farewell.

"Did you love Jerome Meredith?" she asked. Ruth Granger ground out her cigarette and shook her head slowly.

"I don't know," she said. "I often wonder."

Miss Pomeroy started out of the room, but Mrs. Granger abruptly called her back.

"How long would it take to save a thousand dollars if I could get a job?" she asked.

"Some women might do it in two years," Miss Pomeroy

said, "but I doubt if you could."

"Thanks, then; I'll stick to blackmail," Mrs. Granger said.

The friendly butler guided the nurse to the front door; having reached it, on a sudden impulse she darted back to the library and gave her hostess five dollars. "For incidentals," she said, and trotted back to the front door before thanks or a refusal could be issued.

In the taxi and on the train back to town she tried hard to assemble all the facts she had into a coherent whole. Mrs. Granger had undoubtedly contributed a piece toward the solution of this puzzle. That she could obviously just as well have contributed two or three was annoying but didn't necessarily detract from the value of the one. That the one could fit in so many different ways was tantalizing, of course, yet it was only to be expected at this stage of the story. It was like a little piece of blue sky in a very large jigsaw—blue sky that might turn out, after all, to be water.

The first obvious deduction was that Ruth Granger's story exonerated Doris Meredith. If Ruth had been locked out of the Meredith apartment on the night of December 3rd, she had certainly not stood by inside and watched Doris shoot Jerome. But this simple conclusion was based on the premise that both Ruth and Doris were telling the truth. If either one were lying the conclusion was quite invalid, and if both were lying the possibilities were dizzying.

The second obvious deduction was that Ruth Granger herself had not committed the murder. That one seemed to stand up better under analysis, and Miss Pomeroy felt reasonably well satisfied that she had eliminated one suspect. As Jerome's mistress, Ruth was certainly a suspect. However, if she had murdered him she would almost certainly have tried to find some other way to secure a thousand dollars than by reopening the closed case with an admission that her alibi for that night was false. On the other hand there was a possibility that she was a psychopathic exhibitionist or a plain fool, and had reopened the case precisely because she was the criminal.

Miss Pomeroy sighed and tried again. Supposing, for the sake of simplicity, that both Doris and Ruth were telling the truth, they two were eliminated. In that case Doris had left the apartment with her husband in normal health and spirits, her child just being put to bed, at about eight o'clock. Miss Pomeroy drew a small notebook from her purse and wrote in a fine, precise hand:

1. What time did Mr. Fortune call for Mrs. Meredith on the night of December 3rd?
2. How long did he stay, and what time did he and Mrs. Meredith leave?
3. What time did Mrs. Granger come to the apartment? (N.B. Mrs. Meredith thought she saw her outside as she herself was leaving. Therefore it is probable that she was already waiting, and went upstairs almost immediately afterward.)

She closed the notebook and leaned back, shutting her eyes so that she could concentrate better. If Mrs. Granger had come upstairs almost immediately, the murderer must still have preceded her, for the only possible explanation for her having been locked out was that Jerome Meredith was engaged with his executioner. But if she had been sitting in a taxi watching the house until the coast was clear, she must have seen the murderer enter the building. Miss Pomeroy opened her eyes, and then sighed and shook her head. That wouldn't do. Mrs. Granger could not have been sitting in a taxi all that time, or she would never have dared to testify that she had spent the evening at home on Long Island. A taxi driver would be sure to remember a fare who had acted like that. On the other hand, last December she had still had a car of her own. It might very well have been possible to sit quietly at the curb in it and watch. But if she had done so, she must know more of the murderer than what she overheard at the door. Moreover, Dick Fortune as well as his sister was eliminated as a suspect by this sequence of events. She opened the notebook and wrote again.

A. Dick comes for Doris.
B. They leave together.
C. Murderer goes up. Query—Why did Mrs. Granger wait?
D. Mrs. Granger goes up while murderer is still in apartment.
E. Mrs. Granger comes down. Query—Did she drive away immediately?
F. Doris phones home; gets no answer. Query—Was murderer gone?

G. Murderer leaves—(either before or after F)
H. Doris comes home, looks in nursery only. Jerome is
   dead in living room.
I. Doris goes back to theater.
J. Doris and Dick come home from theater together,
   and Doris discovers the body.

There was another possibility, underlined by this analysis with a sinister likelihood. If the murderer had not needed to go upstairs and back down, two excellent chances to be seen could have been skipped. Miss Wright was in the apartment all the time. To pull a trigger and then swallow a sedative—or even to swallow a sedative and then pull a trigger—was by no means difficult. It would be a dangerously thin alibi, of course. And there was the more serious objection that all the trained investigators who had worked on the case had been able to discover no connection between Miss Wright and Jerome Meredith. Young women didn't murder their employers of one week for no reason whatever.

What sort of man had Jerome Meredith been, Miss Pomeroy wondered then. How would he have treated a young girl left alone in the apartment with him in the course of her work? No one, so far, had really thrown very much light on his character. It began to seem pretty obvious that the next step, after reporting Mrs. Granger's offer to Mrs. Meredith, was to talk to Miss Wright. And now Miss Pomeroy's spirits began to soar again; perhaps she was getting somewhere after all.

She telephoned from the station; Dr. Owen was not at his office nor at his apartment. After a moment's hesitation she tried the Shelton and called for Mrs. Meredith.

"Miss Pomeroy speaking," she said, when Doris's voice came over the wire. "I'm just back from Long Island. I've been talking to Mrs. Granger. I wanted to tell Dr. Owen what I'd found out, but I can't reach him, so perhaps I'd better tell you directly."

"Oh, he's here, Miss Pomeroy," Doris said, "he and Dick, too. Do come and tell us; I want you to meet Dick anyway; he's so grateful to you both for what you're doing for me."

"I don't know if I should," Miss Pomeroy said.

"Of course you should. Come over right away. We'll be waiting for you."

Miss Pomeroy's still susceptible feminine heart fluttered a little at the sight of young Richard Fortune. No other young man, of course, was quite so handsome, so brilliant or so charming as Dr. Owen, but Mr. Fortune ran him a close second. His resemblance to his sister was striking, although he was very tall and she very slight. The three of them were sitting in easy chairs in the reception room of Doris's suite, with glasses in their hands, when Miss Pomeroy came in. They all stood up, and Mr. Fortune stepped forward without waiting to be introduced.

"Dr. Owen and my sister have been telling me all that you and he have done for her," he said impulsively. "I haven't any words to thank you."

"We haven't done anything, Mr. Fortune," she said.

"I'm only grateful that you don't think we're officious."

"Good Lord, no! Has that woman been giving you a rotten time this afternoon?"

"Not at all. It was quite interesting. She wants you to give her a thousand dollars, Mrs. Meredith."

Doris set down her glass, and the color drained from her face. Too late Miss Pomeroy realized the implication of the demand thus baldly stated. She hurried on to repair the damage as best she might without giving Doris's secret away to her brother. "She says she was at the door of the apartment that night. She—she had a key, but she couldn't get in. The latch was set. But she heard something. She thinks perhaps you would be willing to give her the money to know what it was she heard."

Doris still looked dazed.

"I don't believe a word of it," Dick said violently. "It's sheer blackmail."

"It may be," Miss Pomeroy agreed. "She needs the money dreadfully." She sketched Ruth's situation to them briefly. "I didn't find out as much as I should have when I talked to her," she confessed, "but on the way home I figured out some things that may perhaps be useful." She drew out the little notebook and showed them her lists.

"Don't you think the next thing to do is talk to Miss Wright?"

"I've been wanting to for two months," Dick said, "but Doris wouldn't let me."

"Let Hillis do it," Doris said, through white lips. "He has a better chance than either of us of getting to her without starting an awful row. And, oh, Hillis, do manage without upsetting her if you can—and try to get a glimpse of the baby."

"I'd like to see your lists before we break up," Dick Fortune said politely.

"What are your questions? Shoot." The doctor grinned at her.

Miss Pomeroy handed her notebook to Dick.

"I can answer 1 and 2," Doris said, looking over his shoulder. "Dick didn't come up that night at all. He was delayed, and he phoned me to be ready and meet him in the lobby. We saved five minutes that way, and just reached our seats as the curtain went up. As for what time Ruth came to the apartment, if she came at all, I have no idea."

"That's a good point," Dick commented. "If you saw her as we were leaving, she must have gone up immediately afterward. And yet she tells Miss Pomeroy that when she went up the door was locked—and implies the murderer was inside."

"But that would have to be Betty," Doris said.

"Unless it was Ruth," Dick reminded her grimly. "Are you going to give her the money?"

"Why of course not," Doris said. "I wouldn't dream of it. Would you?"

"It never hurts to know all there is to know," he said, "but I guess you're right at that. It wouldn't do to fork over anything that could be made to look like blackmail. I'll take her letter, by the way, Miss Pomeroy. We may be able to use it."

Chapter 5

DR. OWEN drove out to Brooklyn the next afternoon without previously announcing his intention to the object of his call. It was quite possible that the senior Mrs. Meredith would not be willing to let him in at all, and the chances of getting to talk to the nursemaid were probably better if he gave her no opportunity to consider his application. He turned into a street of respectable detached houses, each in its own small plot of more or less tidy green lawn. It was easy to see that Jerome Meredith had climbed several steps up the social and financial ladder from the starting point furnished him by his family background—easy to understand, too, how readily jealousy of the superior ease and grace of the Fortune's way of life could sprout in this soil.

Hillis Owen parked his car and walked up the wooden steps that led to the front porch of a brown frame house bearing the number he wanted. A child's velocipede and a doll bed on the porch contributed to his conviction that this was the right house, and reassured him about the welfare of Adriana. There was something agreeably relaxed and homelike in the untidiness of the scene. The woman who came to the door in answer to his ring was less reassuring. She was an elderly woman wearing a house dress. Her gray hair was untidy and she was wiping her hands on a kitchen apron; obviously she was not prepared for unexpected callers. Her face, through the screen door, was hard and suspicious; she looked as if she thought Dr. Owen was selling something which she was quite sure she didn't want to buy. A quick glance at the car parked at the curb brightened her up perceptibly, but she still stood defensively inside the screen door.

Dr. Owen took out one of his professional cards, not without trepidation. He had planned his approach, but now that he was here he was not at all sure that the plan was a good one.

"I wish to talk with Miss Betty Wright, if you please," he said, trying to sound pleasant and yet as firm and assured as possible, "in connection with the Meredith murder case."

The woman took the card and read it. Then she opened the screen door without comment, shouting over her shoulder into the interior of the house:

"Betty! Here's a man from the Coroner's office wants to talk to you."

Hillis opened his mouth to correct this misapprehension, and then closed it again. He hadn't presented himself under false colors; if people wanted to make mistakes, that was their business.

The elderly woman gestured toward a chair in the drably furnished living room, and Dr. Owen seated himself gingerly. She sat down also, but made no attempt to carry on a conversation. There had been no response from Betty. After a moment the doctor said uneasily:

"You are Mrs. Meredith, I presume?"

"Yes, I am," she said, "and nobody has any idea what this all has meant to me. A mother's heart, you know,

Dr. er"—

"Owen," he supplied.

"A mother's heart," she went on, without acknowledging or seeming to have noticed the interpolation. "Jerome was the best boy in the world to his parents; he never gave me a moment's trouble in all his life, and then suddenly this, and the terrible trial and all the things they said about him. No one knows how terrible it all was for me. My husband is very sympathetic, but even he doesn't understand. It is a marvel to everyone that I survived, Dr. Umph, I have a very weak heart, and many's the time my son said to my husband: 'She'll never live through this, not with her heart.' "

"Remarkable," he said. "And I understand you're keeping his child too. Isn't that a good deal of a task for a woman in your delicate state of health?"

"I'd do anything for Jerome's baby," she said, "anything. She's all I have left. I'll never give her up."

There were running steps on the stairs, and Miss Betty Wright appeared at this moment, furnishing a welcome interruption. She was a slim, pallid fair-haired youngster with a strained, tense expression that Dr. Owen noted professionally. Offhand she didn't look like the best person in the world to have the care of a sensitive child recently subjected to several severe emotional shocks. She was wearing an immaculate white uniform with a flowered handkerchief tucked into its breast pocket, and there was a bright red ribbon in her hair, but she didn't look as if she had added these ornaments for the sake of Dr. Owen.

"Aren't you ever going to let me alone?" she burst out,

without waiting for an introduction. "Is this to go on forever? Just because I happened to be there that night, must I be tortured all of my life?"

"I hope not, Miss Wright," the doctor said gravely. "I'm very sorry to have to trouble you again." He glanced at Mrs. Meredith, who sat still looking mournful but interested. "I think perhaps I ought to talk to you alone," he said. "Would some other room be more convenient, Mrs. Meredith?"

"Oh, no," she said. "I can tell when I'm not wanted. I'll leave you. I have work to do anyway. Where's Adriana, Betty?"

"Sleeping," the nursemaid said briefly, without taking her eyes from the doctor. When Mrs. Meredith had gone, closing the door ostentatiously behind her, she burst out again: "You're torturing me, all of you, and I can't endure it much longer. I was only doing my work. I don't know anything. How can I ever get another place now? Why can't you let me alone and let me forget?"

"Please try to control yourself, Miss Wright," he said. "I'm very sorry to have to bring this up again. First I ought to tell you that Mrs. Meredith was mistaken. Unhappily I'm not from the Coroner's office. I'm investigating the murder privately, and so far as I know there is no official investigation underway now."

He paused, half expecting the girl to turn him out of the house, but having once accepted his authority she evidently found it difficult to realize that he actually had none. He thought of telling her he came from Doris, and then discarded the notion. The girl looked unstable, even if she were really friendly to Doris, and moreover he had a fairly strong suspicion that Mrs. Meredith was eavesdropping.

"There's really only one question to ask," he said kindly. "Now that you've had time to think it over calmly, away from the police and the courtroom, are you still certain that you have absolutely no idea how you could have taken a sedative that night?"

Her answer astonished him so that, experienced as he was, he was hard put to it to maintain his composure.

"He gave it to me," she said, bursting into a storm of tears. "Now you know will you go away and let me alone? I never did anybody any harm. I never said it was Mrs. Meredith; they tried and tried and tried to make me, but I never would. I thought I was saving myself trouble saying I didn't know, and you've hounded me to death and now will you let me alone?"

He let her sob noisily while he went back through the story of the murder in an attempt to fit in this piece of information. This was sleuthing with a vengeance. Two days, two interviews, and he and Pomeroy had each picked up a valuable item that had entirely escaped the police. Could it be too good? Had the girl reached the point where she would say anything that she thought would stop questions most quickly?

"I wish I could promise you would be let alone now, Miss Wright," he said quietly, "but you realize yourself that you made a serious mistake in concealing this important evidence for so long. And the more fully and freely you talk to me now that you're ready to tell the truth, the better my chance of protecting you from more questioning."

"There's nothing to sound so dreadful about," she said. "He gave it to me; as soon as Adriana was in bed he came in and asked me to have a drink; I told him I never drank, and he kidded a little and said it was just a light wine and would be good for me and I needed to complete my education. He made me go in the living room and sit down and drink it; he kept kidding all the time; he was nice. And then he said it wasn't so very dreadful, was it, and I didn't feel drunk, did I, and I said no, only sleepy, and went back to my room to bed. And the next I knew they had me at the police station, shaking me and making me drink awful coffee and stuff, and that stomach pump, and I was scared, and I said I didn't know how I got it. But I never said Mrs. Meredith gave it to me; they promised to let me alone if I would, and I didn't, I didn't, I didn't, and I never will. He was a nice man and he didn't mean any harm, and I didn't hurt anybody; I never said she did it."

"You were foolish not to tell the truth, but you showed excellent self-control and consideration," he said judicially. "If you've done any harm, this has fixed it up, I think. I'm going away now in just a few minutes. Are you sure you've told me everything?"

"That was all. I was asleep when it happened."

"There was no one else in the apartment when Mr. Meredith gave you the drink?"

"Nobody. I've told you and told you, we were all alone."

"And you didn't hear anyone coming as you were falling asleep?"

"That's all I know, I tell you. It's all; it's all."

"Stop that," he said sharply. "You're responsible for the health of a small child away from its mother; you've got to hold onto yourself better than that."

"I will," she sobbed. "Only don't ask me any more about it. I want to forget it now."

"I have no more to ask you," he said, "and if you've told me the truth, there will be little more need for anyone to bother you. But you will have to establish your self-control so that you'll be able to testify if the case is reopened. No one wants to hurt you, but we can't help the fact that you are an important witness."

She cried on without answering.

"Is the little girl well?" he asked, hoping to get her mind off her own trouble.

She nodded, sniffling. "I want to get her back to her mother," she said. "She isn't happy here, and neither am I. Young Mrs. Meredith was always good to me. I don't like it here; if it wasn't for Adriana I wouldn't stay on. But she's got no one but me, and I won't leave her."

"I think you'd better go up and wash your face, then, so that she can't see when she wakens that you've been crying. That's upsetting to a child. Thank you for what you've told me; remember you've done right at last, and try not to worry."

"Thank you, sir." The girl stood up, wiping her eyes, and went slowly out of the room and up the stairs.

Mrs. Meredith reëntered immediately. Hillis had been

quite right about the eavesdropping, and she was so angry that she made no attempt to conceal what she had been doing.

"Lies," she said. "Lies, every word of it. She's in with the Fortunes; I've known it all along. All they wanted to do was blacken the name of my poor dead boy. What would he want to do such a thing for, so they could kill him and she wouldn't hear? Doris Fortune killed him, you mark my words, with that precious brother of hers to help. And they paid that girl to lie for them. I never wanted to keep her here; she's no good to me. Not one stroke of work will she do around this house but take care of that child; says she's a nursemaid, not a cleaning woman, if I ever ask her to lift a hand. I don't need a nursemaid to help me take care of one little girl; I leave that to gadabouts like Doris. Why, for that money I could get a good strong housekeeper to make life a little easier for me. I never trusted that girl, but Clifford said to keep her on, to make Adriana happy. The lawyer thought it would look better, but as soon as I have legal control over the child, that two-faced harpy gets out of my house!"

After one or two half-hearted efforts to speak, Dr. Owen made no further attempt to stem the tide. There were items of information floating in this torrent of words that might be of use to Doris.

When at last Mrs. Meredith ran down, he said: "I'm sorry you think the girl is disloyal, Mrs. Meredith. Of course I can see how it looks to you—and yet I'm inclined to think she's telling the truth. She did keep it to herself for a long time; give her credit for that. Of course I know that for Adriana's sake you'll refrain from open quarrelling—but I wish you could feel kindly toward her, too."

"Feel kindly toward her for robbing my dead son of his good name?"

"So many people are suffering in this dreadful business, you have all to be tolerant of one another, haven't you?"

"Nobody thinks about me though." She sniffed and applied her handkerchief. "I'm his mother; nobody else could possibly suffer as I've suffered, and does anyone care?"

Dr. Owen got up precipitately; he had had all the weeping women he could handle for one day, he thought. This was worse than the office.

"I do assure you of my sympathy," he said formally. "And I appreciate your help. I can see that you're very thoughtful of Adriana. Not many women would keep on a nursemaid they personally disliked for the good of the child." The bit of flattery was going to work, he thought. She bridled and muttered that she hoped she knew her duty, and the doctor left with feelings of mingled elation and alarm.

He was certainly getting forward with the investigation. This threw a different light on everything. On the other hand, he had undeniably stirred up a hornet's nest. Doris was determined to do nothing that could hurt the child while the senior Merediths kept her. She would be considerably disturbed if she knew the full story of the result of his interview.

Yesterday Pomeroy thought she had established the innocence of both Ruth Granger and Doris Meredith. Now the pointer swung back toward the two of them.

With the information Pomeroy had picked up yesterday, Meredith's action was perfectly consistent and comprehensible. He had expected Mrs. Granger, and he had deliberately arranged that the nursemaid should be asleep when she came. It didn't make Jerome Meredith sound like any more attractive a character than he had previously appeared, but it fitted. The way it fitted was disagreeable, however. It was straining coincidence too far to believe that the murderer had simply happened on an occasion when the only witness was conveniently out of the way. Whoever killed Jerome Meredith must have known about the sedative he had administered to Betty Wright.

On the face of it, that left three choices. It could have been Doris, and the whole arrangement was horribly consistent with her version of the murder. It could have been Ruth Granger, the one person absolutely certain to know that Meredith had attended to the maid. And it could have been Meredith himself, considerately rendering the girl unconscious before committing suicide. Dr. Owen made a mental note to investigate the suicide possibility more fully. He was accepting the verdict of the police investigators that it was impossible, and already developments made clear that the police were woefully at sea in several respects. If Betty Wright herself had murdered her employer she might have concocted some such story as this. But in that case she would probably have told it sooner. There could be no harm, nevertheless, in checking into her past record to make certain that she had really not known the victim before she was employed in his household.

Dr. Owen swerved sharply to avoid a truck, and wished

that he had the facilities of a police department at his disposal. Following up all these lines with the amateur assistance of Miss Pomeroy was a real job. Of course Dick Fortune and Doris herself were ready to help, but neither of them was in a position to do much.

By the time he had slid through city traffic, parked the car and walked rapidly into the Shelton, elation was again on top of his emotional confusion. He admitted to himself ruefully that much of his pleasure came from confirmation of his previously held opinion that Jerome Meredith must have been a heel. He paused briefly at the desk to ask for Doris, knowing that she was waiting for him. But the clerk brought him up short.

"Mrs. Meredith has gone out to Westchester," he said. "She wants you to call her there, Dr. Owen, at—"

"Never mind," Hillis said, "I know the number."

He hurried into a telephone booth. Had anything gone wrong? Doris had promised to wait for him.

A woman's voice answered when the connection was established. "Mrs. Meredith?" he asked, knowing that the question was ridiculous. It didn't sound in the least like Doris; it was a light, vague voice, and he knew, before the answer came, who it was.

"This is Mrs. Meredith's Aunt Fanny," it said. "She's on her way out here now."

"Oh, I see," he said. "Perhaps I'd better call back. She left word at her hotel for me to call her there. This is Dr. Owen."

"Of course, doctor, she's told us about you and we all appreciate what you are doing so much, but do you really think it's wise, it's caused this trouble already and goodness knows what will happen to the poor girl now, not to mention the baby, and Doris upset and if you do find who it was it can't bring Jerome back to life, thank goodness for that, but I didn't mean to start arguing with you before I even met you, only I'm upset myself too and we none of us know what to do."

"But Miss—Aunt Fanny (what the heck was the woman's last name?) I don't know yet what the trouble is."

"I'll take it, Fanny," another woman's voice said, and then spoke into the telephone in a firm, controlled, well-modulated accent. "This is Mrs. Fortune, Dr. Owen," she said. "Doris should be here very soon now. She's anxious to talk to you. Mrs. Clifford Meredith—the elder one, that is, Doris's mother-in-law, called her a little while ago to say that Miss Wright left the house in Brooklyn just after you did, without leaving any message."

"The hell she did!" Hillis exploded. The old harpy had probably driven her out. And the girl was almost hysterical, in no shape, certainly, to take care of herself. "How did she know she hadn't just run down to the corner drug store?" he asked quietly.

"She couldn't be sure, of course. But just after you left, Betty made a telephone call. Then she went back upstairs, and a little later Mrs. Meredith saw her walking down the street with her hat and coat on and an overnight bag in her hand. She hadn't heard her leave the house, and the girl hadn't said a thing. Mrs. Meredith called after her, but she broke into a run and didn't look around, and there wasn't a car there to go after her. She left some of her things, but all her valuables and all her toilet articles were gone. It really does sound as if she had left without notice, Dr. Owen."

"Yes, it does," he admitted. He could feel his heart dropping like a lead plummet through the mathematical center of his body. What a colossal bit of bungling! This had torn it, right enough.

"Are you there, doctor?" Mrs. Fortune asked anxiously.

"Oh, yes indeed," he said. "Just kicking myself quietly. I'll come right out to the house, Mrs. Fortune. I know Doris will control herself, but please try to persuade her that the child is *really* going to be all right. The grandmother loves her, I'm convinced of that, and what I saw of her toys and things looked quite homelike and comfortable. I'm sure Mrs. Meredith will see that she doesn't suffer. But I'm horribly ashamed of my part. Tell Doris I'm coming just as fast as I can get there."

He hung up the telephone, and turned out of the booth, cursing bitterly under his breath. He took more than one chance with the speed laws enroute to Westchester, but he was lucky. "Good Lord," he thought, "an hour ago I was thinking this was my lucky day."

Hillis Owen had undertaken a serious investigation in a somewhat light-minded spirit, but he was neither a fool nor irresponsible. The full weight of what he had done appalled him. As he approached the Westchester house he wished ardently that he didn't have to face any of them. Doris wouldn't have a word of reproach for him, but the others might not be so tactful. He hoped that they wouldn't; if Dick would bawl him out he might be able to find some justification for himself.

He located the house, parked his car in front, and walked unhappily up the flagstone walk profusely bordered with petunias. Dick Fortune opened the door. He wasn't going to bawl him out, the doctor saw. His face was grim and tired but friendly.

"Nice of you to take the time to come out for a confab," he said. "Maybe we're all making a mountain out of a molehill. Come in and meet the family."

Dr. Owen shook hands with Mrs. Fortune, a handsome, dignified suburban matron in her fifties, and with Miss Scott, who fluttered on the verge of tears. She wasn't little as he had expected, but fully as tall and buxom as her sister. Given any similarity in character they might even have looked alike.

"No more news, I suppose?" he asked when the greetings were over.

Doris shook her head.

"Do you think it at all likely that Mrs. Meredith turned her out?" he asked. "She seemed about ready to. I thought I had that fixed up before I left, but maybe not."

"If she had, I think Betty would have called me," Doris said. "I am still paying her wages. If she couldn't reach me by phone in town she surely could get the house out here."

"Yes, I'm afraid so," he agreed.

"I suppose I should care about the girl," she said, her voice quivering, "but to tell you the truth, all I'm really worrying about is Adriana."

"That's simple," he assured her. "Your mother-in-law

said that she was keeping a nursemaid on against her own
wishes because she thought it would look better when the
custody proceedings got into court if she had done everything that you would for the child. If you're paying the
wages it's even easier. Call her up—your brother'd better
do it—and tell her she must get a substitute from an agency
you select. Then call a good agency and tell them your
requirements. She'll do it, I'm sure. You've got her scared.
And after all, Doris, the very fact that she wants so much
to keep the child proves that she loves her."

"It proves she hates me," Doris said in a low voice.

"She hates that girl," Hillis said briefly. He outlined
what Betty Wright had told him, the story that had caused
him such jubilation earlier in the day.

"I suspected it," Doris said.

"Why in heaven's name didn't you tell me so?" Dick
demanded.

"There didn't seem to be any use. I hadn't any proof.
It would have looked like a shabby way to get out of being
suspected myself."

"Listen, Doris," he said in a voice of strained patience.
"Even if I weren't your brother, as your lawyer I deserve
your full confidence. I can't do anything for you if I don't
have it. What else have you been concealing from me?"

"But, Dick, it was only the thinnest suspicion. I had
nothing to go on except knowing Jerome."

"Well, as it happens I knew it too. But I couldn't use
it on my knowledge alone. Jerome told me once that he
was in the habit of doping the nursemaid when he wanted
to entertain women in the apartment on occasions when

you weren't there, Doris. It was the reason I wanted you to get rid of Emma. I didn't think he'd try it on a new one. But how could I bring that out in court if no one else knew it? It just wouldn't have been believed."

"He told you that?" Hillis asked incredulously.

"You see? Even you can't believe it. There's no good in raking over dead ashes, but my late brother-in-law was a good deal of a bounder."

"But what did you say?"

"I laughed. You can't afford to give a man like that the satisfaction of getting angry at him."

"That's all finished now," Hillis said, "but what happens to that girl is my responsibility."

They looked at him in surprise, all but Aunt Fanny, who said: "But of course, that's what I've been telling you all along."

"You all read detective stories for fun," he said. "That's what got me into this mess; I always thought I was pretty good at figuring them out. Well, you know how the great detective always is, brilliant, erratic, intuitive, way beyond everybody else. When it looks absolutely senseless to other people, he claps himself on the head and says: 'Of course, I see it all now. How stupid of me not to have understood sooner!' Then he doesn't tell what it is he understands, but goes on acting mysterious for a hundred pages more. And then the murderer strikes again, and he says: 'Tut, tut, I should have foreseen that. Awfully careless of me.' But he doesn't foresee the next one, and he goes on acting brilliant and intuitive until half the people in the book are dead." He groaned and put his head in his hands. "Well, that's exactly what I've done to this poor girl."

"You don't mean you think Betty Wright's been murdered?"

"I don't know," he said, making no attempt to soften the truth for Doris. "I have no idea. But look what I do know. She gave me a vital piece of information that she's been keeping to herself. It fits in with the murder somehow. The murderer must have known that Jerome Meredith had doped her. It narrowed the problem down to finding out who could have known that."

"Doris could, Dick could, Mrs. Granger could, the girl herself could, a tramp could," Aunt Fanny interrupted— "a tramp watching his chance to break in could have seen it all through the keyhole."

"Fanny, how could a tramp get into the building?" Mrs. Fortune reproved her sister somewhat shortly.

"A burglar, then, a burglar or a tramp, I don't see that it matters. Burglars do get into apartment buildings, it's very common. I've never been able to see why you people weren't willing to admit it could have been a burglar."

Beneath that vague, fluttering exterior, Miss Scott was tied up in very tight emotional knots, Dr. Owen observed in passing.

"We'll have to leave all that now for awhile," he said. "The thing is to find this girl before any harm comes to her. If the person she called up after I talked to her was by any chance the murderer, she's probably in grave danger."

"Ought we to notify the police?" Doris asked.

"No use," Dick said. "They'd enter it on the blotter

and let it go. Girl walks out on job. What is there to be excited about there?"

"Just the same I'll have to find her," Hillis said. "I could never forgive myself if any harm came to her through my interference. I'm cancelling all my appointments at once, and I'll spend my full time at it until I locate her."

"We'd much better get a good firm of private detectives," Dick said. "Pardon me if I'm rude, doctor, but we have no reason to think you could do any better at finding her than you did at questioning her."

Hillis recognized the edge to the voice. "I deserve that," he said. "I intend to hire detectives. But I intend to go to work at it myself, too."

"Don't you young people quarrel, now," Mrs. Fortune said. "You need to work together. I think you're being unnecessarily dramatic, doctor. You probably frightened her, and she ran away to avoid further questions."

"I hope so," he said, "but I don't dare let it go at that."

"Let's go back to the city together then, doctor," Dick said. "I know a firm of detectives we can get hold of out of office hours and start on this right away. But I really do think you'd better stick to your practice."

"Thanks, but I couldn't put my mind on my practice until I'd helped to find that girl," Dr. Owen answered obstinately.

Chapter 6

BEING a woman was a state popularly supposed to have no disadvantages in the twentieth century, but during the next few days it seemed to Doris Meredith that she was as useless to herself and those she loved as a human being well could be. Dick was in charge of her case for the custody of Adriana, and he called the elder Mrs. Meredith and bullied or cajoled her into accepting another nursemaid of Doris's selection. Doris herself went into town to the agency to interview applicants, and felt for an hour or so that she was doing something useful. But, the candidate once selected, there was nothing more to do. Hillis Owen had clung stubbornly to his announced intention of closing his office while he joined the detectives in the hunt for Betty Wright. Doris missed him more than she liked to admit to herself. In woman's immemorial fashion she sat and waited, listening for the telephone, watching for the mailman, playing cribbage and double solitaire with Aunt Fanny in the evening. On the third morning there was a letter with the address typed on a plain white envelope with no return address. Doris's heart performed a quick somersault as she ripped it open and looked for the signature. It was as she expected, Hillis Owen, in a bold, sprawling hand. The letter was typed too, somewhat inexpertly. Doris smiled at the thought of Dr. Owen's big hands fumbling at a portable typewriter in his lap. But her smile faded as she read.

Dear Doris, the letter began: *I am making some progress, nothing I can tell you as yet, unfortunately, but I am definitely on the track of something. I would give a great deal to come and talk to you, but it is absolutely impossible for me to leave the trail I have picked up, and I believe a letter is safer than the telephone. I don't want* to alarm you, my dear, but I must warn you that the ramifications of the plot in which you are involved are beginning to frighten me. I know you won't be hysterical, for you must depend on yourself now. I think you are in danger, Doris, and I don't know from what quarter. I don't want anything to happen to you, and I have worked out a plan that will protect you unquestionably if—and this is a big if—you will rely entirely on yourself and me, and confide in no one. I mean literally no one, not Dick, your mother, your Aunt Fanny. I shall not tell Pomeroy. I want you to read this letter very carefully, until you are certain you have memorized its contents, and then destroy it.

"Bad news?" Mrs. Fortune asked from above the percolator.

"Disappointing," Doris said, folding the letter and slipping it back into its envelope. "It's from Dr. Owen. He says he hasn't found out anything he can tell us, but he thinks he's making progress."

"It looked to me like quite a long letter to say no more than that," Aunt Fanny said querulously. "Did you finish reading it? What does he say that your old Aunty can't see? You're not flirting with that young man, are you, Doris, and your husband not cold in his grave?"

"Jerome's been dead more than six months, Fanny," Mrs. Fortune said, "and Doris is a grown woman and entitled to keep her private letters to herself if she likes."

Doris was tempted to hand it over to her mother. She felt both of them waiting for her to say: "But of course mother can read it." It took will power to sit quietly and

go on eating Martha's superlative blueberry muffins. There
was no use frightening the poor old souls again after what
they had been through these past few months. Doris felt
that her fingers and toes were cold; she wondered how
long it would be before she could escape to her own room
to finish reading her letter. Aunt Fanny sniffed audibly,
and even mother looked a little offended, but she went
on reading her own mail without further comment. Doris
ate on quietly. Martha's blueberry muffins tasted like
sawdust, but she finished two before she asked to be ex-
cused. She kept from running on the stairs, and she locked
the door against Aunt Fanny's possible impulsive intru-
sion before she reopened the letter. She read the opening
paragraph again, and then went on.

*Just now I can think of only one place where you will
be absolutely safe. It's a small private asylum upstate near
Wampsville. I know the doctors in charge very well; they
are excellent men, and perfectly discreet. I am making all
arrangements to have you admitted as a patient. You will
be guarded day and night as no police department could
possibly protect you. I can get to you at any time, and no
one else can. Let me repeat, Doris, it is vitally important
that you tell no one where you are going. You will have to
make up your own excuse to offer your family.*

*I see all the objections to this scheme, but, my dear girl,
please believe me when I say that in the light of what I
have discovered, they are trivial. I can keep this matter
altogether secret; it need never appear on your medical
record, and if by some fantastic chance it should ever leak*

out, I will be on hand to testify that it was not a genuine commitment.

This is what you must do. Make a good excuse to your family, so that they won't be alarmed if you are gone as much as a week, or even two, if that should be necessary. Pack the fewest essential articles on which you can possibly get along. Get in your car without any waste of time, and drive to Wampsville. I enclose a map showing how to get from there to Glenview Lodge. Carry it with you after you destroy the letter; you must arrive without having to make inquiries by which you could be traced.

At Glenview you will need no identification; tell the gateman your own name and that I sent you. From that point on, everything will be taken care of for you. Please believe that I am sorry to be so mysterious, and that I wouldn't do it unless it were absolutely necessary. And if you have any doubt at all about the wisdom of following my instructions, remember, Doris, that Adriana needs you.

Doris sat still and stared at the big, straggling signature. She was trembling so that the letter shook in her hands. This would never do! She had no question about following the instructions; she trusted Dr. Owen completely. But could she trust herself? Could she make an excuse that would stand the scrutiny of Aunt Fanny's aroused suspicions? Could she find her way without leaving any trace? And could she, all alone, face the terror of this way out? It was a foolish, childish, illogical fear, but the thought of being shut in an asylum, even one that called itself Glenview Lodge, made her scalp prickle and chilled her heart. But even worse than that was the dreadful suspicion at which the letter hinted. Don't tell anyone, not Dick nor your mother, nor your Aunt Fanny. That could mean that everyone who knew her whereabouts offered the murderer one more chance of finding out, or it could mean that Dr. Owen thought he would find the killer among these three who were dearer to her than everyone else in the world except Adriana. Mother? Dick? Absurd. Aunt Fanny? Absurd too. Absurd, of course. Aunt Fanny wouldn't hurt a fly. But Aunt Fanny mustn't know where she was going.

The best lie was one that kept as close as possible to the truth. She remembered that from Dick's childhood instructions. She'd better tell them, then, that she was going into town to help Dr. Owen, and might not communicate with them for a week or two. She must tell them this morning and get away; she couldn't chance standing up under Dick's cross-examination if he should come out today.

She reread the letter slowly and carefully. Could she be sure she had all the instructions clearly in mind? Better not destroy it just yet; save it for one more reading after she had packed and was feeling less nervous. Action of any sort was always a help. Pack the minimum essentials. She got out an overnight bag, and put in toilet articles, nightgowns, lingerie, a couple of sweaters and skirts. It wasn't likely that Glenview Lodge was a dressy place. One black dress, though, and she'd wear a linen suit. With a washable sports dress or two that ought to do her for a couple of weeks. It was like packing to go to the hospital when Adriana was born. She smiled faintly at the thought.

It was good to think, even briefly, about something else than Dr. Owen's letter, and what it could mean. Why must he be so mysterious? Surely it couldn't have done any harm to give her some hint of the direction in which he thought the danger might lie. And how could there be any danger? It was ridiculous. Someone had shot Jerome six months ago; that was a fact. And now Dr. Owen, who in April had believed she was the culprit, thought that the murderer wanted to kill her too. But why? There was no reason. She and Jerome were perfectly ordinary people; no one could have any mysterious vendetta against them. And she had no faintest idea of how Jerome had been killed, so the murderer's classic reason for striking again could not apply in her case. She had no faintest idea— but could the murderer think that she had? She had thought she saw Ruth Granger outside the house that night—and now she knew that she had really seen her. Her spirits lightened suddenly. Ruth Granger! A terrible thought, of course, but not with the same sort of terror that associated itself with the absurd idea that Aunt Fanny — If Ruth Granger had hated Jerome enough to kill him, it was a hatred born of love. And afterwards she must have regretted it. But her hatred of Doris would be a different sort entirely. If she had stood by and seen Doris tried for murder, in grave danger of her life, without saying a word in her defense, what would she be tempted to do when the trial was over and the danger gone? What must be the effect on a highly emotional character like Ruth's of having murdered with impunity—without even having attracted suspicion? By her own account it would have been the easiest thing in the world for her to do. She was present; she had a key. What the emotional conflict between her and Jerome might have been, Doris had no idea. But if she had shot him, if she had seen Doris accused of the crime—even supposing that she herself had not planned it like that—if she had once accustomed herself to the idea that Doris would be punished for it and had then been disappointed by the acquittal—it all fitted together perfectly. What more natural, since murder was so easy, than to dispose of the chief witness against her, who was also her successful rival?

Doris finished her packing in a rush. Hillis's letter meant, then, that Ruth was diabolically clever—so clever that he wanted to leave no clue by which she might trace her prey. Betty Wright, of course, wouldn't fit in. So far as Doris knew, Ruth hadn't even known of the girl's existence until she heard her testify at the trial. But what if she had? What if Ruth had threatened or bribed Betty into keeping silent? What if they had kept up some sort of connection? After Betty had broken down and told the truth, she might well have thought her safest course was to confess at once to Mrs. Granger. And what had happened to her after that was enough to cause Hillis Owen to tell Doris to shut herself up in an insane asylum without delay! Still it was infinitely better this way than thinking it might be some of her own people. She closed the bag with a rush, put a match to the letter and held it until it was completely burned. She started to drop the fragile ash into the waste basket, then shook her head and carried it instead into the bathroom. When the last trace was washed away, she picked up the bag and ran downstairs carrying it.

Aunt Fanny was in the sun parlor watering the house plants and mother was conferring with Martha over menus in the kitchen. Doris headed for the kitchen, and Aunt Fanny, seeing the bag in her hand, followed her there and stood in the door to listen to what she might say.

"Mother, do you mind if I go back to town?" Doris shied away from the direct lie.

"Oh, darling, are you sure you want to?" Her mother looked distressed. "Dr. Owen thinks you're here; this is where he'll call first when he has anything to tell you. And Dick thought you'd do better to stay out here until he could get things settled for you. And we do get lonely without you."

"I'm sorry, mother. I get restless without Adriana. But it's more than that; as a matter of fact Dr. Owen thinks there's something I can do. I may not write or call for a week or two; it sounds kind of melodramatic, but that's what he suggests, and anything is better than just sitting here waiting."

"Of course, dear, we won't stop you if that's what you want."

"Margaret, that's absurd," Aunt Fanny said sharply. "What can you be thinking of to let the child go off by herself with things the way they are? This is your home, Doris, and I'd think you'd be glad enough to stay in it after what's happened to you away from it, and the

Merediths trying so hard to prove you're not fit to have Adriana; the best thing you can do is stay right here and lead a quiet, respectable life. If I were your mother I'd forbid you to stir one step, and if you have any regard for the opinions of your old Aunty, you won't stir one step even if she doesn't stop you."

Doris kissed her, trying to laugh lightly.

"I'm sorry, Aunt Fanny," she said. "I do love you, but I have to go. Don't worry now, either of you, please. I'll be perfectly all right; I'll be with friends, and I'll call you just as soon as I can. Maybe I can come back with Adriana. Wouldn't that make it worth getting along without me for a few days, Aunt Fanny?"

"Just remember, please, that you're going absolutely contrary to my expressed will and judgment," Aunt Fanny answered stiffly.

"Do come home just as soon as you can, dear," mother said.

Doris kissed her too, and walked out of the house carrying her bag. She backed the car out of the garage carefully, and waved to the two old dears standing on the front porch. She backed into the street, drove to the corner, and remembered to turn left, toward New York. Once out of sight, she swung around the block and headed for Wampsville. It was a beautiful June day; roses and peonies were blooming in the well-kept yards along the highway, and in spite of the fact that she was seeking a dismal sanctuary from an unknown murderer, Doris felt her spirits rising. She loved to drive alone in fine weather. For the first time since Jerome's death she gave way to her impulse for speed; the road was straight and clear, and this early in the morning the traffic was light. She pressed the throttle down harder and harder, exulting in the feeling of the wind in her hair. But she had hardly touched sixty-five before she saw the motorcycle in the rear-view mirror.

"Darn it," she said aloud, dropping to a sedate thirty-five and hoping against hope that it was a delivery boy. It wasn't, and the sedate thirty-five didn't pacify the cop.

"Pull over," he ordered, swinging in ahead of her.

This would complicate things badly; she was driving directly away from New York, and there were sure to be inquiries if she didn't get back in time to answer the summons. She opened her purse to get out her license, trying to act unconcerned. Last summer it had been easy to joke with traffic cops; would she never get over this dreadful feeling of guilt and terror when she met a policeman?

"I was going too fast, wasn't I, officer?" she said with forced brightness. "I haven't any excuse, either; it was just such a pretty morning, and I felt good."

This was an approach that sometimes disarmed them, but this cop merely grunted and opened his book to write a ticket. Doris gave up and handed him her license. He glanced at it, read the description, and then looked sharply at her as if to check it. There was no sign of recognition in his manner.

Doris F. Meredith she signed the ticket with a little flourish. Doctor Owen had been right then. People had forgotten her already, and irrationally she felt a slight

pique that this should be true. Ladies of gentle breeding
weren't tried for murder of their husbands every week,
after all.

"I'm going to be out of the state for a little while," she
said. "When will I have to appear to answer that?"

"You can mail in the amount of your fine if you don't
want to come to court," he said. Doris nodded, accepted
the ticket, and pulled away at a more moderate rate. The
rest of the journey passed without incident. She lunched
at a hamburger stand on the outskirts of Albany, and
turned west. Wampsville was not on a main highway, and
she lost a little time around Herkimer finding the road.
It was late afternoon when she reached Wampsville; she
noticed with annoyance that her gasoline supply was low,
but Dr. Owen had particularly cautioned her not to make
herself conspicuous in the little town. She judged that
enough remained to carry her the few miles to Glenview
Lodge unless she lost her way; in any case, she resolved to
chance it.

The road indicated on her map was not paved. It wound
and dipped through the hills charmingly but confusingly.
The surface was good and the road well kept up, although
it was hardly more than a cart track in width. It was a
lonely road; Doris looked from her gasoline gauge to the
landscape and back. Not a chance to buy or cadge a little
fuel anywhere in sight. If she ran out she'd have to walk
back to Wampsville, and a fine way *that* would be to remain inconspicuous. The shadows were long across the
lonely fields; in the hollows the sunlight was gone completely. Glenview Lodge was supposed to appear in six

miles; Doris had come five and a half, and there wasn't a sign of a habitation in sight. It must be the wrong road; she wouldn't go one inch beyond the six miles, she resolved, but turn at once and head for town. There'd not be much chance of getting in with the gas she had, but she'd cut down the distance she'd need to walk as much as possible. She began to watch for a place to turn, and suddenly there on the right was a drive barred by a high gate of woven steel, and above it a modest sign: Glenview Lodge. Not a glimpse of the lodge itself could be secured in this light through the heavy trees and shrubbery. There was a bell at the left of the gate, but Doris sat still in her car and honked. A man came out from among the trees almost at once, a civil gatekeeper in work clothes.

"I'm Mrs. Jerome Meredith," she said. "I'm expected here, I think."

"Yes, ma'am," he said, touching his cap and opening the gate. "I've been looking for you."

Doris drove in. "I just made it," she said. "I forgot to fill up with gas until I got to Wampsville, and then I didn't want to do it there."

She stopped abruptly. After all, the attendants would naturally suppose she was here as a bona fide patient, and there was no point in disillusioning them. The more she acted like a patient, the safer her retirement would be. The man locked the gate behind her and climbed into the car in a matter-of-fact way. He came to the door on the driver's side, and opened it without asking permission. Doris hesitated momentarily, and then moved over to let him drive. For the first time it occurred to her that it was odd for a patient to come alone, driving her own car. If the man thought so he gave no sign. He shifted easily into gear and drove expertly along the narrow, twisting lane. It dipped through a heavily wooded small valley, and emerged onto a vista of green lawn with colorful flower beds and attractive looking chairs and lounges grouped invitingly. The lodge looked like a big, old-fashioned summer hotel; there was no hint of its real purpose in barred windows or doors.

"What a perfectly beautiful place," Doris exclaimed involuntarily.

"That's what all the new patients says, ma'am," the man replied with a sly smile. Doris felt vaguely uncomfortable.

"I suppose you were surprised to have a new patient come driving alone like this," she said tentatively.

"Oh, no, lots of 'em do," he said. "Anyway, you soon gets over being surprised at anything that happens here." He lapsed into silence, and then added, with a grin: "Funny thing is, the ones that come alone all thinks they can take care of themselves, they can go alone any time they feel like it. But that's a different matter—a ve-ry dif-fer-ent matter." He chuckled. Doris decided she didn't like him nearly so well as she had thought when he met her at the gate.

They drew up at the front entrance, and an orderly in a white coat ran down the wooden front steps and took her bag from the car.

"I'm Mrs. Meredith," she said.

"You're to come right into Dr. Grant's office, ma'am," he told her.

She followed him up the steps in the deepening shadow of late afternoon. The gateman drove her car away out of sight. She walked easily, self-confidently through the big, wide-open double doors. Inside the shadows were heavier, for it was not yet dark enough for artificial light. The entrance hall was a lounge, high-ceilinged and airy, with comfortable chairs and tables covered with an assortment of new magazines. The chairs and couches were all empty now, however.

"Where is everyone?"

"Dressing for dinner now, ma'am," he said. "This way please."

They turned to the right, and he knocked at one of a pair of high oak doors that were immediately opened from within. A starched and pleasant looking young nurse smiled at them.

"Mrs. Meredith," the orderly said. "Dr. Grant wanted to see her at once."

"Oh, yes. Come in, Mrs. Meredith. You can take the bag to Room 10 in A, Cyrus." Doris followed the nurse across a small, carpeted reception room to another heavy oak door. The nurse knocked, and a male voice said: "Come in." She pushed open the door and motioned Doris to go first. Dr. Grant was a big, heavy man in early middle-age. His face was ruddy, and though at the moment its expression was cheerful, its lines were hard. Doris felt again the little chill of fear that had touched her when the gate swung shut behind her.

"Good afternoon, Mrs. Meredith," the doctor said, rising and holding out a big hand. "We're very glad to see you, and we hope to make you very comfortable here. I used to say 'happy' but so many patients thought I was joking that I've had to change the phrase. As a matter of fact we do hope to make you happy too, and the better we succeed the sooner you'll be well."

The nurse had withdrawn and shut the door. This must be the set speech of welcome to a new patient, Doris decided. Evidently not even the nurses were to know her status. Well, she'd do her best to play up.

"You want to treat me exactly like any other new patient, then, Dr. Grant?" she asked as soon as she was sure they were alone.

"Hardly that, dear lady," he smiled. "Every patient is an individual. I want you always to remember that. I want you to feel free to come to me at any time with your problems and anxieties. I want you to believe that I am really your friend."

"Just what—what arrangements did Dr. Owen make for me?" she faltered.

"Dr. Owen?" he asked. "Dr. Hillis Owen? You have consulted him? Good man. Excellent man. We'll certainly call him into conference. You showed excellent judgment there, dear lady."

Doris felt her hand at her throat. Mustn't do that. Mustn't show any sign of panic. If she had ever in her life needed to keep her head, now was the time. Be calm; be concise; be so rational that no one could possibly doubt her sanity.

"Didn't Dr. Owen ask you to admit me here?" she asked in a low, controlled voice.

The look of blank surprise on his face was instantly covered by one of comfortable reassurance, but it had been there; there could be no doubt of that.

"Why, yes, yes, of course," he said. "Everything's perfectly regular. Nothing to get excited about."

"Did he write you or telephone?" she asked.

"Now, dear lady," he said, "this is not a medical conference. I'm merely welcoming you to Glenview Lodge; tomorrow we will have time for a good talk, and I'll begin to find out what I need to know in order to help you. You mustn't start cross-examining me at our first meeting; that's my job, you know."

"Dr. Grant, who sent me here?" she said, rising to her feet. "It's my right. I demand to know."

The geniality dropped from his tone. "Mrs. Meredith, we are all here to help you," he said sharply. "But what we can do for you depends almost entirely on your co-operation. You know that a conviction of persecution is one of the commonest symptoms of your condition. You must try not to give in to it. I assure you that you are safe and well cared for here."

"I'm sure of that," she said, holding on to her control. "But, Dr. Grant, a dreadful mistake has been made. I'm not accusing you of conniving, doctor, really. I suppose a great many of your patients don't think they belong here, and you take that as one more proof of their insanity. But you need to keep an open mind, too. Isn't it possible, doctor, that now and again a patient is tricked into coming here? I have been. I assure you, Dr. Grant, I know what I'm saying. I have been tricked into coming here, and unless you will believe me and tell me who made the arrangements for my admission, there is no chance of my finding out how."

Her voice was rising; there was a hysterical note in its urgency. He sat quite still and stared at her, but the mask of professional reassurance was in its place over his features; she saw that she had not penetrated to his mind at all.

"Your privileges and pleasures here, Mrs. Meredith," he said, "will depend on your ability to rid yourself of hallucinations and to control yourself. You are going first to the quarantine house, where all our new patients spend a few days. Your classification, when you are ready to leave it, depends on you. Before you leave Glenview Lodge you will be able to spend some weeks in this house, where our patients who are almost cured can live a normal life. I hope to have the pleasure of welcoming you here soon."

"Please, doctor," she said, "please listen to me for just a moment without prejudice. So much depends on it. I tell you I have been tricked."

"Mrs. Meredith, one half hour ago you were out there on the open highway, free to go anywhere you chose. If there was a legitimate doubt of the wisdom of your coming here, why didn't it occur to you then? I assure you the reaction you are feeling now is the product of a sick fancy."

"Then, Dr. Grant, I'll try to be a good patient, if you will only answer me one question now. Who arranged to have me admitted here?"

"You did," he said.

Chapter 7

HILLIS drew up at the Westchester house with a little sigh of weariness and looked hopefully at the front door. No sign of Doris. It would be nice to have a few minutes alone with her before he tackled the others. As if in mockery of the notion, the front door flew open and Miss Scott came hurrying across the lawn.

"Dr. Owen," she said, "we're so glad to see you. But she isn't with you, is she? That's a disappointment, but it's something to have you bring us news of her. I do wish you would let her come home; I can't see anything but absolute foolishness in all of this."

"Miss Wright?" he asked. "We haven't found out a thing."

"Well, that's too bad, I'm sorry of course, but I was really talking about Doris."

"About Doris?" he said, and caught himself up sharply.

"Yes, and this nonsense of her going into town to help you and not letting us know where she is. It's absolutely senseless, you know, and when I saw your car I thought you'd realized it and brought her home."

"No," he said, "not just yet. When did she go?"

"The morning she got your letter. The minute she got your letter I might say. Wednesday morning it was, and here it is Friday and no word from her. Where are you keeping her anyway?"

"I'm just on my way into town now," he said. "I thought

she might not have gone yet, and I could give her a lift in. I won't get out, then. Tell Mrs. Fortune I'll send her home as soon as I can."

He snapped the car into gear and started forward almost before Miss Scott had time to get out of the way. As soon as he was out of sight of the house he stopped before a drug store and ran in to a telephone booth. It was a brief enough matter to get Richard Fortune's office; it took a little longer, and some explanations, to get Mr. Fortune himself. The rising young professional man, all right!

"Dick," he said, when the connection was completed. "Hillis Owen. Do you know where Doris is?"

"Why, no. Mother and Aunt Fanny had some story about you being the one that knew."

"So I just gathered. Well, it's a frame-up. I thought she was at home."

The hesitation at the other end of the wire was so brief as almost not to be. Then Dick's incisive voice spoke sharply.

"Get to the Keene Detective Agency on West 43rd as fast as you can. I'll have my office call and tell them we're coming. I'll meet you there. Wait; is there any more you can tell me? I can get there before you do, and perhaps get them started."

"Not a thing. I expected to find her at home. I didn't want to pump your Aunt Fanny for fear of frightening her more. I daresay you know more than I do about what took her away."

"Right. I'll see you at Keene's."

Dr. Owen hung up, and walked back to his car, slowly,

thoughtfully, like a man engaged in deep cogitation rather than like one struggling with sudden alarm. But once in the car he drove as if a foul fiend were after him, and he arrived in West 43rd Street earlier than Richard Fortune expected to see him. He was shown at once into a conference room, and found Dick engaged with a young man who looked as if he ought to be wearing his hat on the back of his head, but wasn't.

"Dr. Hillis Owen, Mr. Keene," Dick introduced them brusquely. "Mr. Keene's just been asking me, Hillis, exactly what your connection is with this case, and I'm damned if I can tell him."

"Why, I'm Doris's friend, acting in her interest, I suppose."

"We can let it go at that for the present anyway. And where have you been spending the past week, Dr. Owen?"

"I've been upstate in Betty Wright's home town playing a hunch that she'd go straight back to her own folks. No soap."

"You knew, didn't you, doctor," the detective asked, "that our men were covering the same angle?"

"Yes, I knew it," he said. "I'd seen the girl and you had only photographs. I thought I might find something you'd miss."

"But you didn't?"

"No, I'm sorry to say I didn't."

"And meanwhile someone using your name has lured Doris away from home to God knows where?"

"That's what I'm told."

"Now, gentlemen," the detective said, "getting excited

won't help. I'll tell you how it looks to me, and nine chances out of ten I'm right. First this girl disappears, right? No warning, just one telephone call and she walks out. Then Mrs. Meredith does the same. This time it's a letter she says was from Dr. Owen, but nobody seen the letter. Notice this, gentlemen. Both girls walked away under their own power. Nobody snatched 'em. Chances of anybody trickin' 'em both are pretty thin. But suppose your sister was getting desperate about her child, Mr. Fortune. Suppose she figured it didn't look like she was ever going to get her back legally, and thought the place she was staying was bad for her. What does a mother do under those circumstances? She tries direct action, of course. Mrs. Meredith is too smart a dame to go and try a dumb snatch that she'd be caught in the act. She frames it up right with the nursemaid. You take my word for it, them two are somewhere together. The way to find them is to put a twenty-four hour tail on the baby. That way you'll catch them red-handed trying to kidnap her."

"Good Lord!" Hillis said. "Would that be kidnapping, Dick?"

"Technically," he said heavily. "The courts aren't likely to be very hard on a mother under those circumstances, though. But it would be a crime, all right."

"Well, for God's sake, then, get the tail on the baby and stop her before she can do it," the doctor said.

Dick shook his head. "I don't think that's the way it is," he said. "Doris trusts me too well to try that over my head. Her custody case isn't in bad shape at all."

"It's the best way to go at it, anyway," the detective

said. "We can't just walk out into New York State and find anybody we got a notion to, you know. We're good, but we ain't that good. All we can do is try all the places they might go or all the people that might know about them, and until we find another line, that's the best chance on Mrs. Meredith."

"Go ahead on it," Dick said. "Whatever happens, don't let her do it. It would be fatal to her case. And follow every other line you can think of. Never mind the expense; we'll stand for anything legitimate."

He turned toward Hillis. "You may remember, doctor, that I tried to dissuade you from leaving your practice to go after the Wright girl. You wouldn't listen to me then. I didn't want to be rude, and I didn't insist. Now I don't care. This is serious; it wouldn't have happened if you'd been minding your own business. I want you to drop the comic sleuthing. This is a job for experts."

Hillis felt his face reddening angrily. "I'm sorry you feel that way, Mr. Fortune," he said stiffly.

Dick looked a little uncomfortable. "If I'm unnecessarily rude now, please remember I'm under a strain. But I'm speaking before Mr. Keene deliberately. I want him to understand clearly that from now on you have no status whatever in this investigation."

"Doesn't Mrs. Meredith's expressed desire carry any weight with you?"

"Look here, Dr. Owen. I don't know one thing about you. I don't know where Doris met you. The first time I ever hear your name she tells me that you are good friends and she wants you to help on this investigation—an investigation that I've been trying in vain for two months to get her to authorize. And now she's gone, leaving word that you know where she is. You say you don't, but we have only your word against hers on that. Put yourself in my place and try to imagine how you'd feel."

Hillis nodded, still stiffly. "I see your point," he said. "Of course I shall welcome any inquiries you may wish to make as to my professional or personal standing."

"We'll make 'em all right," the detective said pleasantly.

"Just for a start, then, where did you meet Doris?" Dick asked.

The doctor hesitated briefly. "I don't believe, your attitude being what it is, that I care to tell you that," he said. "I assure you I have no idea where she is now. I think Mr. Keene will find that I am a man on whose word you can rely."

"If he doesn't, you'll hear more from me," Dick said grimly.

"Good-bye, then," Dr. Owen answered. "You can find me in the telephone book. I hope you'll let me know if there's anything I can do."

"I don't think it very likely," Doris's brother said. "Good-bye, Dr. Owen."

Hillis turned on his heel and walked out of the detective's office, seething with rage. The worst of it was he'd brought it on himself. There was more than a modicum of justice in what Richard Fortune had said. The detective obviously saw him as an interfering fool. And there was nothing in the record so far on which he could pride him-

self that he was anything else. Leaving Doris out of the
question altogether, it was a sorry mess. And he couldn't
leave her out.

As he walked thoughtfully back to his car, the conviction grew in his mind that he couldn't count himself out
of the investigation at Dick's request. If the detective's
guess were right—and there was a good deal of sound common sense in it—he and his men would find Doris, probably in time to prevent her from doing anything foolish.
But if it were wrong, they would waste valuable time in
working on it.

Hillis turned in at the garage where he had parked his
car, and then checked himself on the threshold. Doris
and Dick had spent the evening of December 3rd at a
theater on West 45th Street. All of the garages at which
Dick might possibly have parked his car that night were
within easy walking distance. On impulse he walked two
blocks north and surveyed the situation. There were three
garages in the block. He walked to the office of the first
one, and with an air of confident authority announced
that he was investigating the Meredith murder case, and
wanted to know whether Mrs. Meredith's brother, Mr.
Richard Fortune, had parked his car there during theater
hours on the night of December 3rd. It was ridiculously
easy; the man in the office did not attempt to question the
authority. He said that the garage didn't keep a record of
the names of the theater trade, but that he thought it
likely if Mr. Fortune's car had been parked there that
night he would have heard something about it when the
police were first investigating. He hadn't. Hillis thanked

him and tried the next garage. The man in charge answered equally guilelessly. Yes, Mr. Fortune had parked there that night. They had been over it all with the police. No, they'd kept no record of his name, but with the murder breaking the next day and the police coming around the same week, they'd been able to remember. No, Mr. Fortune had not taken the car out during the performance. Yes, he was absolutely certain. The police had been backward and forward over that point, and checked the possibility of his taking it out without notice. The car hadn't been out of their garage between eight-thirty and eleven-fifteen.

Dr. Owen sighed, gave the man a dollar, and walked away. Of course it was what he should have expected. You couldn't pin a murder on a man just because he'd been gratuitously insulting. And of course if Dick Fortune had taken his car out that night, the police would have known it. There remained the possibility that he had used a taxicab, like Doris. But there was a good deal against it. He would, of course, have taken the precaution of walking a block or so away from the theater, and getting out a block or so from his real destination. And he would have taken one cab to the apartment house and another back to the theater. But even at that he'd have been taking a terrible chance, as the driver's prompt identification of Doris proved. More than that, he had been back in his seat in ample time for the second act curtain. He had, of course, had a head start over Doris. She had taken time to telephone. But even at that, to walk far enough from the theater to be safe, hail a cab, get out far enough from the apartment house to be safe, go up and murder Jerome Meredith, come back out—avoiding Doris—and repeat the performance with the cabs, within the time allowed for an intermission at the theater, was a physical impossibility. No, much as he would have liked to make out a case, Hillis didn't see how Richard Fortune could have killed Jerome Meredith.

He would go back to the office, talk to Pomeroy, arrange to begin seeing patients again. He remembered the keys Doris had given him to her deserted apartment. He'd get them and go through the place. There might be something the police had overlooked. There was plenty to do even if Richard Fortune wouldn't cooperate. He wasn't out of the investigation by a long shot! He quickened his pace back to the garage where his own car was parked.

When he came into his office, Pomeroy was at her desk busy with records. Stiffly starched, tidy, pink of cheek and gray of hair, she was a comforting and familiar sight. She looked up brightly at the sound of the opening door, and smiled with genuine pleasure when she saw the doctor.

"Doctor Owen. It's good to have you back. There are three rather urgent calls."

"I'll look after 'em a little later. Don't you want to know what's happened?"

"You didn't find Miss Wright," she hazarded. She would never have ventured to guess so freely in a professional matter; as a detective Pomeroy evidently considered herself on a par with the boss, and she wasn't so far wrong at that.

"Worse," he said. "I've lost Mrs. Meredith, and you

and I have been gently but firmly booted out of the investigation." He summarized briefly for her what had happened. Miss Pomeroy listened with her usual flattering concentration. When he had finished she said concisely:

"You won't need to lose any more time from your practice, then."

"You don't really think I'm going to give up now, do you, Pomeroy? Leave Doris to her fate, as you might say?" He spoke lightly, but the two lines down the center of his forehead were not light.

"What can you do?" she asked.

"What I'd like to do is call in the police again," he said. "I'm almost sure it's what should be done, but I don't quite have the nerve to do it on my own responsibility. They'll never in the world get Doris by watching the baby. The whole idea's crazy; she has far too much sense. Fortune thought so himself when Keene first mentioned it. Here's a place where the police could do something that a private firm never could. She left home in her car. You can hide a body, but you can't hide a car—not very easily, you can't. Put the police on it, and they'd trace that in a couple of days."

"Why don't you call them then?"

"I'm not sure they'd listen to me. I'm not a member of the family; I'm not even an old personal friend—just the victim's doctor. Particularly if the Fortunes refuse to back me up, I don't believe the police would pay any attention at all."

He leaned over, elbows on knees, and dug his hands into his curly hair.

"Good Lord, Pomeroy, this is ghastly," he said. "The woman's in terrible danger; it's my fault, at least partly, and there isn't a damn thing I can do."

"Maybe she's not in danger, Dr. Owen. There are a lot of reasons she could have gone away. Perhaps she did go of her own accord. She was a bit unstable, you know. And it's not your fault that she used your name."

"Oh, Pomeroy, use your head. Who but her husband's murderer would have any reason to lure her away from all her friends and her family? As for some nutty impulse of her own, I'll stake my reputation as a psychiatrist she didn't do that, any more than she shot her husband. And I wish to heaven I could prove either point." He pondered a moment, pressing his head against his hands.

"Give me the urgent calls," he said at last. "I'll see about them first, and then I'm going to try a little amateur burglary. Dick Fortune doesn't know I have the keys to the Meredith apartment. I don't suppose there's a thing left there, but I may as well take a look."

His professional work occupied him for the rest of the day; when he was ready to put his mind again to the problem of finding Doris Meredith, the late twilight of a summer evening was falling. It would be much more sensible to go to the apartment in the day time, he knew. The electricity would of course have been turned off, and a flashlight had the double disadvantage of showing very little and being likely to attract attention to itself. But with his work finished, he found it impossible to face an idle evening.

"You may have to come to the jail and bail me out,

Pomeroy," he said lightly.

"I'd much rather go with you and be your lookout," she answered. He started to laugh her off, and then hesitated.

"You've been better than I have at this job so far," he said, "but I wouldn't want to get you in bad."

"I don't think it's burglary at all when Mrs. Meredith gave you the keys. And if we were caught, I'd make it look much more respectable."

"You've got something there," he admitted. "Come along, then, Pomeroy. I'm no good without you anyway."

He insisted on taking her to dinner before they began their work. Eating cold salmon and green salad at a sidewalk cafe, they conferred further over the case.

"What do you really think now about the murder, Pomeroy?" he asked her. "I've gotten so concerned over this business about Doris I've half forgotten the original problem."

"It seems to me it's mainly one of elimination," she answered seriously. "I'm pretty sure Mrs. Granger didn't do it and Mrs. Meredith didn't do it. That leaves as possibilities Mr. Granger, Miss Wright, Mr. or Mrs. Clifford Meredith Senior or Junior, or any combination of the four of them, Mrs. Fortune, Mr. Richard Fortune and Miss Scott—unless it was someone of whom I haven't yet heard."

"Good heavens, Pomeroy, you are thorough," he said. "What possible motive could most of those people have —and why are you so certain it wasn't Doris or Mrs. Granger?"

"Different persons, different motives," she answered, taking one question at a time. "Those are all the people I know of as yet who were involved with Mr. Meredith. There may be others. We don't know yet how his money was left. That issue may have something to do with the Merediths' anxiety to keep the child. The only persons I have talked to myself are young Mrs. Meredith and Mrs. Granger. I believe Mrs. Granger told me the truth, and that, of course, lets out Mrs. Meredith as well as herself."

"But what makes you think she told you the truth?" he insisted. "You're not one to play hunches, Pomeroy."

"Why, no," she said. "It's not hunches or intuition or anything like that. Most people can tell whether or not other people are telling them the truth. You can't exactly explain it, you can just tell. Only when it's very important, people are likely to be so careful they doubt their own instincts. But they don't need to. That's all there is to it."

"Then all we need to do to settle this case is to let you talk with everyone involved, get all their stories of the crime, and spot which one is lying."

"Of course that's not so easy as it sounds. The guilty one, especially, won't want to talk to me, but probably a lot of others won't either."

"And when you do find the right one, we'll still have the job of making the police believe you know when somebody is lying to you."

"Not necessarily. Once we find who did it, Mrs. Meredith's mind will be relieved. Maybe it will be somebody that we'd better just let alone."

"You mean you'd connive at letting the crime of murder go unpunished?"

"The crime of murder never goes unpunished. I wouldn't hinder the police, but now they're finished with this case I'm not sure I'd call them in again—not until I knew what I was doing, anyway."

"You're immoral, you know," he said, "and criminal too. But I'm awfully glad you're with me on this adventure."

. They walked east from dinner to the apartment on 52nd Street. Dr. Owen was whistling softly under his breath, a sure sign of nervousness. Miss Pomeroy walked briskly, her face serene and bright.

"Let's walk past the door once," he proposed, "to get the lay of the land. I'd really rather not meet anybody in there, though of course we can't be certain we won't. You be looking at numbers sort of vaguely."

Pomeroy looked for numbers much too high on their doors with admirable vagueness, and the doctor peered sharply into the corridor of 427. It was a standard, characterless apartment house entrance, with bilious yellowish plaster walls and one large potted palm for elegance. There was no one in sight within. They walked two or three houses past their destination, and then, turning as if they had missed the house they were looking for, went back. Dr. Owen fished out Doris Meredith's keys. He slipped one into the lock; it turned readily, and he swung the door open.

"We're in for it now," he muttered, motioning Pomeroy to go ahead. They walked briskly and confidently, like people sure of their destination, into the lobby. The single automatic elevator was well back and to the right. Dr. Owen pressed the button and waited, tapping his foot. This time their luck didn't hold; when the elevator came down two people got out, but they glanced incuriously at the waiting couple and went on their way. Dr. Owen stepped in quickly as they held the front door open for someone coming in; he wanted the elevator alone, so that no one should notice they were getting off at the sixth floor. He shut the door of the cage and pressed the button just in time. The elevator started reluctantly upward with the peculiar, hesitating gait of an automatic elevator, and the doctor explained to Miss Pomeroy.

"We could have walked up, but if we'd met anyone it would have been much more conspicuous than this way."

The elevator stopped at the sixth floor, and pushing back the door, he said: "If we meet anyone here we'll probably have to turn tail and try again another time. There are only four apartments to a floor."

The sixth floor, however, was deserted. Dr. Owen had the key for apartment D in his hand, and wasted no time in crossing the narrow hall, fitting it to the lock, and entering the dark, silent, deserted apartment. Miss Pomeroy stood beside him in the foyer. He noticed that he was himself breathing hard, but she seemed totally unperturbed. Mechanically he clicked the light switch, but there was no response. As he expected, the electricity had been turned off. It was not yet completely dark outdoors, but in here he could barely discern the shadowy shapes of the furniture. He pressed the button of his searchlight, and swept the room with its beam. It was a conventional apartment-house hall, furnished with good taste and modest luxury. Clean and barren now, it had nothing of Doris's personality remaining. On a polished table at his right hand stood an empty silver card tray. A larger table gleamed dully against the opposite wall, bearing a handsome pair of candlesticks. There were six formal chairs ranged exactly along the walls; Doris had mentioned that the foyer was the dining room. A gleaming white kitchen was to the right. He flashed his torch inquisitively into all its corners. The refrigerator was warm, clean and empty, the food cupboards bare. Dishes and glasses were ranged in neat, geometrical rows. He explored the dropped living room next. It was an impressive apartment, with ceiling-high windows at one end, and built-in bookcases of equal height at the other. The handsome rug and draperies were still in place, and the electric beam caught the gleam of polished andirons in the empty fireplace. He inspected it carefully; it was absolutely clean, with not even a trace of dust. The tall bookcases were undisturbed; the chairs and sofas, with smoking and coffee tables and reading lamps conveniently at hand, were in stiff and correct order.

He noticed a secretary, and tried the desk door. It was unlocked, and gave to his touch. It still contained papers. They were arranged in neat piles and had undoubtedly been looked over before this. He left them without a closer glance.

Back up to the foyer and into the bedrooms. The first

would be the master bedroom, large and comfortable, with solid, masculine-looking furnishings. A bed, a chest of drawers, a dressing table. He opened the drawers, one after another. Nothing. The bathroom was an empty waste of lavender tile. The nursery was smaller than the master bedroom, and here most of the furniture had been removed. The senior Merediths had evidently taken Adriana's possessions along with herself. The nursery had its own bath and a large dressing closet containing a cot; doubtless this was where Miss Wright had slept on the night of the murder. Even without a sedative she was pretty well cut off from the activity of the apartment.

He sighed and leaned against the window. Not a trace of occupancy. To this very moment he had hoped against hope that he would find Doris hiding here. It was quite probable that she would have another set of keys than the one she had given him, and if she needed to hide she would be hard put to it to find a safer or more legitimate retreat. There wasn't a chance, however; no one had been living in this apartment for some weeks.

"I thought Mrs. Meredith might be here, Pomeroy," he said heavily. "I hardly know what to start looking for now she isn't."

"Yes, I know," she said. "That's why you wanted me to come along, so you wouldn't frighten her. Well, now we're here you'd better search the place."

"Of course," he agreed without enthusiasm.

The job was quickly done. Bureau drawers, linen chests, bathroom cabinets, were already empty. The living room rug had been cleaned or changed; there was no spot on this one. The chair in which Jerome Meredith had been sitting when Doris and Dick found him was probably gone.

Hillis went slowly through the papers in the desk, while Pomeroy systematically removed books from the lower shelf of the bookcase, shook them out and returned them to their places. The papers in the desk were characterless —receipted bills, a Line-A-Day Diary that had belonged to Jerome Meredith, an engagement pad with cryptic notations, an address list headed "Christmas Cards." Doris had never sent those Christmas cards. Dr. Owen stuffed them all into a brief case he found in the living room closet. He could make more of them at his leisure at home. He turned his attention then to helping Pomeroy with the books. It was a big job, but it was the best chance in the place of finding something.

Two hours of hard work netted a card from a rental library, a shopping list, an eighteen month old wedding announcement and a set of genealogical papers about the Fortune family. There were notations in Doris's hand, Hillis noted. He hadn't known she went in for that sort of thing. He added all these documents to the pile in the brief case.

"Guess we'd better call it a night, Pomeroy," he said reluctantly. "I never knew sleuthing was as hard work as this."

"You ought to move every October first the way I do," she answered cheerfully. "It keeps you in trim."

Chapter 8

GOING through the papers he had abstracted from the Meredith apartment was even harder work than securing them in the first place, Dr. Owen discovered over the week-end. Where, he wondered, had the legend ever started that it was an amusing business to read other people's letters and diaries? He disposed first of the bills. They were all receipted and all reasonable—clothing, toys, liquors, cigars, food, rent, electricity—the ordinary, legitimate expenses of a well-to-do small family. There was nothing there. The engagement calendar he took more slowly and laboriously, for many of the notations were in a sort of personal shorthand. As he deciphered them, however, they all proved innocuous and pointless. It was Doris's, evidently, and listed bridge and luncheon dates, committee meetings, appointments with the hairdresser and with a doctor. Hillis thought he had stumbled on something there, but investigation proved the man was a pediatrician. The calls were doubtless routine check-ups on Adriana. The list of names and addresses headed "Christmas Cards" included the Grangers and the younger Clifford Merediths. Hillis scrutinized the list thoroughly enough to convince himself that it was what it purported to be, and put it aside.

Jerome Meredith's line-a-day diary was obviously the most promising document he had found. But it was even more disappointing than the others. It was a discreet record, clearly written in the consciousness that it might be read by hostile eyes. It was an odd thing for a busy and successful man to keep, Hillis thought. The entries were schoolgirlish in their triviality; there was no reference to business, and each day's record was too short to serve as any form of self-expression. Mr. Meredith had evidently been on a diet; there were brief notations as to what he had been eating and how he felt in consequence. There were also, Hillis realized as he read on, a good many references to a certain R, presumably Mrs. Granger. They were all brief and non-committal, but they added up. Could it have been left in the desk at home deliberately, Dr. Owen wondered, in the hope that Doris would read it? Was it meant to flaunt the affair with Ruth Granger in her face, but so carefully that no third person could use it against Jerome?

Sept. 5—Lunch with R. Cocktails and lobster. No bad effects. This diet all guff anyhow.
Sept. 8—Flowers to R. No message. She will understand.
Sept. 10—Remembered just in time this was Doris's birthday. Cancelled dinner date with R. and took Doris out.

But surely the police had not overlooked all this? Pomeroy, whom he consulted on the Monday, was, as usual, ready to supply information. No, indeed, the police had not overlooked the diary. Mrs. Granger had had a very uncomfortable day on the stand, but she had come out of it with flying colors. There was nothing that could be proved beyond flowers, books, candy and luncheon dates.

On the evening of the murder she had been at home with her husband on Long Island; their testimony concurred on that point.

So there was nothing new in the diary. Hillis sighed and turned to the genealogical notes. Not the sort of pastime he would have supposed Doris would care for, but there was a good deal of her handwriting on the pages. It was the usual stuff, tracing the Fortune family back to the Mayflower. There were quite a respectable number of substantial and useful citizens among Doris's forbears—governors, senators, judges, a signer of the Declaration of Independence. The great-great grandfather of Dick and Doris had been another Richard Fortune. Hillis glanced idly through his record, and then stiffened with surprise and looked more closely. He had been quite right; there, in Doris's fine, delicate hand was written *d. insane 1847*. There was no comment. Richard Fortune had been a considerable landowner and successful speculator in western lands; he had lived for a time in Ohio and Missouri, and had come back east a rich man. He was the father of five children, dignified head of a family, and then, suddenly, *d. insane 1847*. Hillis leafed back through the other pages and read more closely. But there was nothing either before or after him to throw any further light on the history of Richard Fortune, b. 1800, m. Adriana Van Rye 1825, d. insane 1847.

Why in the world hadn't Doris told him? The fact in itself was not half so sinister as her silence. Plenty of thoroughly normal people could find insanity in the family four generations back. But when she had come to him as a psychiatrist, with the story she had brought him, why should she have suppressed so obviously pertinent an item in her family history? She might have thought that the insanity of a great-great grandfather was a negligible matter, if neither his forbears nor his descendants had repeated the strain. Or, more probably, she had been ashamed to admit it. People were funny about such things; it was a quirk he was always encountering in his patients. But he wouldn't have thought it of Doris.

He leaned back in his swivel chair, his head thrown back, his long legs stretched out before him in an attitude he favored when he needed to think. His thoughts were not pleasant. Psychiatry remained a mysterious science with vast unexplored areas. The judgments of an expert in that field were not necessarily irrevocable. He had told Doris that he believed she was sane; he had believed she was sane. But putting the pieces together one by one —the dreams, the hallucinations, the mysterious disappearance entirely of her own volition, and now the great-great grandfather whose tragic illness she had been ashamed or afraid to admit—Hillis groaned, and put his head in his hands. It was his problem, too. No use trying to fool himself; he loved the woman. He had thought more than once of asking her to marry him. If there had been only this, he'd still have been willing to chance it. But this on top of all the rest—a man who had seen what a psychiatrist sees couldn't wish that on his children.

Dr. Owen pulled himself sharply erect. At the moment Doris's life might be in the balance, and he sat here mooning over his feeling for her like a lovesick schoolboy. He

drew toward him across the polished desk the neat scrap-
book of clippings of newspaper stories about the trial
which Miss Pomeroy had arranged for him, and read attentively. The suicide question was definitely answered.
According to uncontested expert evidence, Jerome Meredith had been shot from a distance of at least ten feet. The
gun was farther than that away from the body. There had
to be a murderer then. He read on for an hour—an hour
that represented days and weeks in a gloomy courtroom,
where a straight, gallant little figure held all eyes. He
pushed it away at last, unable to read any more.

He knew well enough what the next step should be.
It wasn't particularly pleasant, but at least he could go
in his own person, with no bluffing about imaginary
authority.

"Get me T. A. Granger's office," he said to Miss
Pomeroy. "I want to speak to Mr. Granger himself. If
they insist on knowing what about, you can mention Mrs.
Meredith's name."

"You haven't opened your mail, doctor," Miss Pomeroy
said. "Shall I go through it for you?"

Hillis glanced through the accumulated envelopes. All
familiar business, nothing that could possibly be from
Doris.

"Yes, will you?" he said. "Answer what you can and
mark the rest for me."

Half an hour later he was sitting in a comfortable leather
chair looking across a polished desk into the unfriendly
eyes of Thomas Aquinas Granger.

"I'll have to ask you to come right to the point, doctor,"

Mr. Granger was saying with cold civility. "I'm afraid you're wasting your time and mine at best. I understand you want to see me on some matter concerning Mrs. Jerome Meredith, and I can assure you I have no connection whatsoever with that lady's affairs."

"You don't, for instance, know where she is now?"

"Why, no." Mr. Granger was on guard, but momentarily he appeared to be genuinely surprised. "Where should she be?"

"She has been with her mother and her aunt. I'm her physician; she left them saying she was coming to me, and she hasn't been heard of since."

Mr. Granger raised his eyebrows. "She's of age, isn't she? She struck me as a young woman who could take care of herself. Perhaps she won't thank you for raising a hullabaloo."

Dr. Owen kept his temper. "We're afraid there's been some dirty work," he said. "It's not impossible it was connected with her husband's murder."

Mr. Granger shrugged slightly and distorted his features into a grimace plainly indicative of doubt.

"Of course if the family wants to report it to the police, that's their privilege," he said. "It's not what I'd do in their place. As for your question, doctor, you could just as well have asked it over the phone. I haven't the slightest notion where Mrs. Meredith is, and I don't greatly care."

"And Mrs. Granger?" Dr. Owen kept his voice carefully casual, but at the look on the face of the man opposite him, he braced himself for a blow, and it was with difficulty that he restrained himself from ducking.

But Thomas Granger did not hit him. After a momentary struggle with himself he answered in a voice thick with rage.

"There was nothing I could do about the police dragging my wife into a dirty murder trial. But I don't have to sit still and let a lot of foul-mouthed strangers continue the game. You can leave here right now, Dr. Owen, if you care to leave in one piece."

Hillis Owen thought it highly probable that the threat was more than bluster. He didn't care for physical affrays; he was tempted to leave as requested. But having come this far he might as well accomplish something if possible. It was tough, he reflected, not knowing whether he had to deal with a murderer or merely a bad-tempered man who could control himself when the necessity for control was obvious. The technique of handling him would be quite different in the two cases.

"I didn't come here to libel Mrs. Granger," he answered slowly, without moving from his chair.

"If you try, you can answer for it in court," the other man interrupted.

"However," Hillis said, "just before Mrs. Meredith disappeared, Mrs. Granger was trying to get money from her."

Thomas Granger hadn't known that. But the access of murderous rage was quickly followed by calculation; he hadn't known it, yet he believed it now.

"How?" he asked. "On what grounds?"

It was Dr. Owen's turn to shrug. "I haven't come here to gossip. If I tell you things you hadn't known about your wife, it's with a definite purpose. You'd better talk over the details with her yourself."

"All right, I will. Let's get to your definite purpose."

"I want to find Mrs. Meredith. I thought it very likely you or your wife might know something about her. I still think your wife may."

"And if she does?"

"If she does, you'd better persuade her to tell Mrs. Meredith's family at once. Here's the situation, Mr. Granger. Mrs. Meredith has decided, very recently, to press the investigation into the true circumstances surrounding her husband's death. The only reasonable explanation for her disappearance is that someone who is afraid of that investigation has spirited her away. But that was a stupid and useless thing to do. The investigation is hydra-headed. Mrs. Meredith's brother, and several other people, know all that she knew about the facts, and are even more determined than she was to press the inquiry. Anyone who harms Mrs. Meredith is absolutely certain to make things worse for the murderer of Jerome Meredith as well as for himself."

"You make yourself unflatteringly clear, Dr. Owen," the big man said softly.

"I'm glad. I hoped to. Incidentally, several other persons, whom I shan't bother to name, know as much as I do about Mrs. Granger's attempt to touch Mrs. Meredith. We shan't broadcast it, any of us, but we sort of protect each other, if you see what I mean."

"I do see."

"Moreover," Hillis continued briskly, "assuming, for the moment, that you have no guilty knowledge of the murder, you're making a great mistake in your treatment of your wife."

As the wave of angry red swept again over the big face the doctor thought professionally: "He'd better watch his arteries." But he hurried on to say what he had to say, forestalling interruption.

"You can't punish any human being by putting him in an intolerable situation unless you're prepared to take the consequences. That's not an easy thing for an angry person to understand, but it's important. It's the reason we'll go on having wars for several centuries to come; the victors can never remember that simple fact when it comes time to write a peace treaty."

"I'm not interested, Dr. Owen, either in sermons on pacifism or advice about my private affairs."

"But your quarrel with your wife is no longer a private affair; if it were I shouldn't be here. That's just the point I'm trying to make. When the pressure is too great, there's bound to be an explosion in some direction. I don't know or care anything about the reasons for your disagreement. But you'd better make up your mind either to give her a divorce or to live with her again on reasonable terms. If you don't do one thing or the other, I'm warning you that you're in for trouble."

He stood up. "You needn't ask me again to go. I'm leaving. I shan't try to talk with Mrs. Granger. You're in a better position to find out what she knows about Mrs. Meredith; if you get any information you had better call Mr. Richard Fortune here in town. And—er—Mr. Granger —you can't get away with doing your wife any violence, you know. If anything were to happen to her I should go directly to the police. In fact, if I decide on sober second thought that I've put her in any danger I'll go directly to the police from here. I'm not going to cause another murder."

"Get out," Thomas Granger said.

Dr. Owen left without further exchange of pleasantries. His next step was a matter for cogitation. He was beginning to have more sympathy for the detectives of fiction who slapped themselves on the wrist after each murder of a star witness. What he ought to do next depended entirely on the temper of Mr. Thomas Granger, and that was an unknown quantity. To go to the police and ask them to protect Ruth Granger if she didn't need it would be the act of an officious fool, a gratuitous public washing of other people's dirty linen. But if he failed to do it and anything happened to her his folly would have been even more serious. It was a hard question to decide. Granger was vindictive and could nurse a grudge; his revenge on his wife proved that. But it proved also that he was calculating; witholding money from her was an act of mean cruelty that could not react on him. The impulsive rage that led to physical violence was another matter.

A compromise solution occurred to him. He could go over and confess to the Keene detective agency what he had just done. It had its drawbacks; his opinion of the competence of the private operators was not unduly high, and it would be awkward to admit that he was still concerning himself with the case after the slap Dick Fortune had administered there. On the other hand, the situation was well within the limitations of their power; he could even order, on his own responsibility, that a bodyguard should be sent out to the house for Mrs. Granger. It was the thing to do.

He looked about him. The entrance to the Astoria-Corona-Flushing subway was half a block away, beside the public library. He could duck in there, shuttle across to the West Side, and be in Keene's office before he'd have time to get his car out.

That was another idea, he thought, running down the steps into the subway. Often enough it was a much faster means of transportation than a car or taxi; could Richard Fortune have taken a crosstown subway to the Meredith apartment between acts on the night of the murder? He laughed at himself for the way that question of Richard's whereabouts during the entreacte continued to nag at him. Every other person remotely connected with the case could have been at the apartment during the evening; there wasn't a watertight alibi in the lot. You could make a list headed Opportunity and put everybody on it—everybody but Dick Fortune. And wasn't it always the perfect alibi that cracked in the end? However, if Dick's were going to, the subway wasn't the answer. West 45th Street—three blocks down to 42nd to the shuttle entrance, across town to Grand Central, a couple of blocks underground there to catch an uptown east side local, off at 51st Street and a couple more blocks—nobody but Dick Tracy could do that in an intermission.

Dr. Owen roused from his musings to the realization that he had struck the subway in the first stages of the evening rush hour. He hesitated, on the verge of turning back, and then dropped his nickel and pushed through the turnstile. Wouldn't do him any harm to rub shoulders with the common people once in a while; the rarefied atmosphere of a Park Avenue office could be bad for a psychiatrist who needed to know all about human nature. There was plenty of it down here, with all the attendant smells, noise and pushing. Dr. Owen elbowed his way forward to the edge of the platform, gaining in the process something of the emotional release furnished by a good game of football.

There was a train coming; the roar and the glare of the lights were so menacing that he pushed back another inch from the edge of the platform. He pushed back against a solid wall of human beings who had not succeeded in edging into spots quite so favorable as his, and almost instantly there was an answering push forward. "That fool should watch out," Hillis Owen thought, and before he could brace himself he was hurtling over the edge onto the track. The roar and glare of the onrushing monster overwhelmed him, but his past life did not unreel in his mind like a motion picture. Instead he felt only a murderous rage and the single, thwarting thought "Now no one will ever know who did it."

He heard himself scream and a horrible cacophony of screams; he tried to grasp the front of the car, to be carried along with it and not ground beneath it. He heard a roar and a grinding crash, felt an impact, and saw a great constellation of light.

Chapter 9

THE first week Doris Meredith spent at Glenview Lodge passed like a nightmare. The comparison, she thought, lying awake on her narrow white iron cot on the eighth morning, was much more accurate than such comparisons usually are. Lying with her eyes open she could see the white canvas curtains of her cubicle in the Quarantine House; when she closed them the events of the past week danced crazily before her. And yet none of it had been so very dreadful in itself. The horror came from the terrible sense of being lost in a waste of utter confusion. There was nothing, no one, to cling to. The trick which had brought her here had upset the values of her whole world. There was no one she dared trust, and worst of all she could not trust herself.

She had behaved, she realized now, very badly. Stunned by what had happened, and terrified by what it might portend, she had taken refuge in silence, refusing to talk to any of the doctors who tried to interview her. Of course that looked bad; she knew it perfectly well. But what could she say that would make a better impression than silence? Even now to try to reason it out brought back the terrifying vertigo. For whatever questions she asked herself came back always to the one central, dreadful, inescapable one. Was she actually a victim of her own delusions? Had she voluntarily made arrangements for her own admission to this place, and then forgotten? It was a theory that fitted with so many of the facts. If it were the right one she ought to submit herself to treatment, answer their questions, be docile and obedient, try to cooperate in curing herself.

But it wasn't right; it wasn't; it wasn't; it wasn't. As always, the certainty came rushing back, sweeping the doubt away as a rolling wave washed footprints out of sand. She pounded with one clenched fist on the counterpane, and then forced herself to stop and lie still. If she weren't hysterical, if she behaved in every way reasonably and sanely, surely they would see in a little while that she was all right and listen to her story. But what if they wouldn't? What if they were in a conspiracy against her? That was what insane people always thought, but couldn't it happen? The days when people were shut up in insane asylums by treachery were ended; every intelligent person knew that. The law today put every safeguard around commitment. Vaguely she remembered that it required the signatures of two doctors, examining independently, as well as of the next of kin. And there was something called the Lunacy Commission you could appeal to. But here she was; she hadn't been committed; she had never interviewed any doctor except Hillis Owen—and here recurred the most appalling, the most hideous notion of all. Maybe Dr. Owen had found her insane and had been too tenderhearted to tell her so. Perhaps the trick that had sent her here was actually of his invention, and had been played for her own good. If they would only tell her anything. She battered her head continually against their bland, yielding, kindly stubbornness, like a lunatic battering literally against the walls of a padded cell.

One thing at least was certain. Glenview Lodge was an expensive private sanitarium; as long as she remained here someone was paying her bills. She had tried to bargain with the doctor for that information. Tell me who's paying for me, and I'll answer all your questions. They treated the inquiry indulgently as a vagary, and smilingly refused to answer. Surely if the place were legitimate, if they were not conniving at a trick to keep her captive, they would be willing to answer that question.

But during the night she had decided at last what she must do, and it was foolish to let her mind continue going around and around in this treadmill. She believed she was sane; she believed she had been tricked, and now she must prepare to act on that belief. If it were right it must mean that she was completely at the mercy of her husband's murderer. No one else could possibly have had any motive for luring her away from her family in secrecy. And now no one else knew where she was, but the murderer knew—and whenever he chose to strike she was there at hand, defenseless. Cold sweat broke out on her forehead at the thought. Calm, calm, she must be calm and collected. She was alone against the world. There was no one she could trust—no one, here or outside. She must escape. That was obvious. And having escaped she must still rely on herself, must remain alone and hidden until she had unraveled this hideous mystery and regained Adriana.

Adriana was the one thing she must not think about until all this was behind her. The first step in making ready for escape was to cooperate with the attendants. Make them believe she was resigned to being here so that they would allow her some freedom. It wouldn't be easy; they were used to the cunning of insane persons. But she must try. Be patient, be wary, but don't be afraid. Slow and easy. She mustn't try it until she was sure she could do it. Being caught in the attempt would end all hope forever.

A nurse came in with a basin and a jug of warm water.

"Good morning, Mrs. Meredith," she said briskly, professionally.

Doris forced her lips into an answering smile.

"Good morning," she said. It was pretty feeble, but it was an improvement over sullen dumbness.

The nurse looked slightly startled and definitely pleased, but she made no comment. After a moment Doris herself underlined the response.

"I'm feeling much better this morning, nurse. Miss—?"

"Gregory," the nurse said. "That's splendid. Dr. Eamon will be delighted."

"I'm afraid I've been a great trial to Dr. Eamon," Doris confessed. "I'll be better from now on. Do you suppose I can talk to Dr. Grant again?"

"Dr. Eamon is keeping in very close touch with Dr. Grant about you, you may be sure. We want all the patients to feel that they have access to headquarters at any time," Miss Gregory smiled evasively.

"Yes, but do they?" Doris thought without speaking. There were times when the habit of silence was valuable.

"I hope after I've talked with Doctor Eamon today he'll be willing to let me have my clothes and get out of this." Doris plucked at the heavy white hospital gown. Miss Gregory looked at her sharply, and she wondered if she had gone too far. Surely it was natural for a woman to want her clothes back for other reasons than to escape.

She washed herself and arranged her hair without help, as she had done every morning of this week. She couldn't bear the thought of having any of the attendants touch her. Waiting for breakfast she sat propped up in bed looking at the narrowly circumscribed vista of trees through her small, high, barred window. It was impossible to see anything that indicated the layout of the grounds or any means of escape. One thing was certain; she must get out of this house before she could even consider getting clear away. The main lodge, she was sure, had not had barred windows; if she could behave well enough to be assigned to a house where she would be allowed a reasonable amount of freedom, she could survey the situation and make her plans. Just how to behave with the doctors was still a problem. If she were a prisoner here for some nefarious purpose, pretending to be resigned would only put them on their guard. But if they really believed she was a bona fide patient, docility was the best way to gain some degree of liberty.

She ate all of her breakfast when it came, and hoped that the hearty meal would improve her color. There was no mirror in the cubicle, but it was not hard for her to imagine what a week of sleeplessness and nibbling at her meal trays had done to her appearance.

Her effort did some good; she could see that as soon as young Dr. Eamon came in for his morning visit. She was sitting up in bed, her hair arranged to the best advantage she could manage without a mirror. He did not, like the nurse, mask his surprise and pleasure, but whistled and grinned at her.

"Well, well, well, Mrs. Meredith," he said. "Feeling better this morning, aren't we? I heard something about that."

"Much better," she said. "And I'd feel better yet if I could have a bed-jacket and some rouge and hairpins."

"All in good time, young lady," he answered smiling. "Take it easy is our motto here, you know."

"Yes, I know," she said, "and from now on I'm going to try to follow it."

"Why the transformation?" he asked lightly, still smiling.

"I want to get out of here just as fast as I can," Doris said. That was another thing Dick had taught her in childhood. When you need to make a lie stick, tell the truth just as far as you can. The longer you can stick to it, the more convincing your eventual lie will be.

"Bad as all that? What's wrong? Meals? Nurses? Me?"

Doris gestured to the barred window. "I don't like that. It makes me feel shut in."

He was considering her, she could see, as a psychiatrist and not as a human being. He did not smile at her last remark, and Doris made a mental note not to joke any more.

"Well, you won't be here much longer," he answered consolingly. "None of us like bars, and we won't keep you behind them a minute longer than necessary."

"That's fine," she said. "I'm sorry I've been behaving so stupidly. I'm going to be a good patient now."

"Splendid," he said. "Now let's listen to that heart again."

Doris submitted quietly while he applied his stethescope and took her blood pressure.

"You ought to know a good deal about me by now, with all the tests you've been making this week," she ventured.

"We do," he smiled. "Practically everything. The way things look this morning, Mrs. Meredith, chances are you can get out of quarantine today. I'm not quite sure where you'll be assigned, but I think you'll like it better than this."

"Shall I have to stay in bed?"

"I don't think so."

He went on about his rounds, and Doris lay back on her cot, feeling better than she had since last December. Now at least she was doing something, however slowly. In the end she would extricate herself; she was sure of it.

At noon Miss Gregory came in with a suitcase in one hand and the linen suit over her other arm. Doris felt her heart leap with delight.

"You're to dress and see Dr. Grant in his office this afternoon, Mrs. Meredith. And then I'm afraid this is good-bye; you're ready to be assigned to a permanent house."

There was an ominous ring to the word "permanent" that Doris didn't like, but she made no comment. She dressed with all possible speed, and when she was ready to do her hair, Miss Gregory held a hand mirror for her. She held it, Doris noted, well out of reach, so far, in fact, that it was hard to see herself in it at all. But she was able to make herself look presentable, and walking across the grounds toward Dr. Grant's office in mid-afternoon she felt entirely mistress of herself.

The place was beautiful; there was no denying that. She looked about her at the green lawns and flowering bushes with a cautious but genuine pleasure. There was no sign here of any fence; the grounds were extensive. She remembered the fence through the gate in which she had entered as being about ten feet high, with the top curving inward. She couldn't remember whether or not there was barbed wire on top. She thought her best chance was probably climbing. She retained from childhood an agility at the sport. The only other method that occurred to her was to find where visitors' cars were parked and conceal herself in a trunk on some visiting day. This was such a simple and obvious means of escape, however, that she doubted whether the patients could get across to visitors' cars. If they could, the trunks and tonneaus were doubtless kept locked. And last and most serious of all, even if she could get outside the walls of Glenwood Lodge in such a fashion, it would still be an awkward and difficult matter to get out of the trunk without being observed and arrested. For the present she was willing to watch and wait.

Dr. Grant was seated at his big, shining desk when she came in. His ruddy face was smiling genially, but Doris felt more strongly than ever that she could not trust the man behind it. She seated herself and waited, warily, for what he might say, sensing a trap behind every word.

"Ah, dear lady," he said, "I'm glad to see you again. Very glad to hear you're beginning to feel a little happier with us."

"Thank you, Dr. Grant," she said.

"Ready to believe we're your friends now? We can't help you, you know, until you'll help us."

"I know it, Dr. Grant. Yes, I'm ready to help. I'm still a little—confused—over just how I came here, but I'm sure you'll be able to help me straighten it out. Have you consulted Dr. Owen about me?"

"Little delay there. We haven't been able to get in touch with Dr. Owen just yet. The best thing you can do, dear lady, is go over the same ground with us that you have with Dr. Owen."

She fought down her bitter disappointment. "There isn't much to tell," she said slowly. "Since my husband's death I've been sleeping badly, and I have terrible dreams. Until I came here that was really all. Then there was this confusion about coming here. I thought Dr. Owen asked me to come. I still don't have it quite straight."

She rubbed her forehead wearily, and beneath her hand kept sharp watch to see the doctor's reaction to what she said. He seemed entirely satisfied with it and unsuspicious.

"Don't worry," he said. "I dare say you had quite an emotional struggle deciding to come here at all. You've just been through the reaction, and from now on you can expect to improve steadily. Now about your dreams—"

Doris made a hasty mental selection from those of her unpleasant dreams which she considered least informative, and began to relate them.

Her afternoon was so far successful that when she left Dr. Grant's office she went back to a red brick building, much larger than the quarantine house, and somewhat less alarming in general appearance. There were no bars at the windows, and Doris was shown to a private room with an attractive chintz-covered couch and—joy of joys—her clothes neatly ranged in a shallow closet. The decoration of the room struggled unsuccessfully to be attractive and restful and at the same time strictly utilitarian. There was no mirror; the clothes in the closet hung from wooden pegs; the glass windows were high and deeply recessed, and there was no possible way to climb up to them, as every article of furniture was anchored to the floor as if this had been a ship's cabin. The few toilet articles ranged on the dressing table included nothing that could by any possibility be used as a weapon.

Doris looked critically at the nurse who came to help her get settled. She was a middle aged woman with the professional cheerfulness of all the attendants.

"Isn't this a cute little room, Mrs. Meredith?" she asked. "We hope you're going to be very happy in here."

"What I'm really looking forward to is getting out," Doris said pleasantly, with a frankness she hoped was disarming.

The nurse smiled. "Very right and very proper. That's what we're all trying to do here, you know—work ourselves out of our jobs."

She disclosed the few secrets of the little apartment and indicated the location of the bathroom. "You won't be upstairs very much anyway," she said. "We lead a very busy and very regular life here; you'll come to your own room at night and for a daytime nap, but most of the time you'll be busy in the public rooms."

"Doing what?" Doris asked.

"You'll be surprised," the nurse whinnied. "Sports and handicraft and music—we have a good library. Maybe you can be in the dramatic club. There's never a dull moment here."

Doris discovered that she disliked this woman very much. If she were going to try to bribe any nurse, it had better be one in whom she sensed some sympathy. Not that there was much chance anyway. She had nothing with which to bribe except promises, and they were doubtless cheap here.

She ate her dinner at a long refectory table in the big dining room without conversation or any attempt to notice her fellow patients. Her own load of trouble and anxiety was all she could shoulder just now, she felt, without burdening her mind with the tragic stories of these others. No one disturbed her; a new patient who preferred to eat in sullen silence was evidently no novelty. After dinner there was dancing in the lounge; the nurse insisted that Doris should take part in this, and she did, unwillingly, saying nothing to her partners, but noting over their shoulders the ring of watchful attendants.

The routine of the next day fulfilled what the nurse had promised about it, and demonstrated as well that Doris could not expect one waking moment to be free from supervision for the weeks to come.

"At least it's a protection," she thought. "No one could possibly murder me with all these people watching."

Hard physical exercise was a part of the therapeutic program, and for that Doris was very grateful because it meant that she could condition herself for the difficult days that must follow her escape. Simply to get out of these walls, with no clothes but those she stood in and without a cent of money was far from being enough. She was gradually elaborating a plan as she watched her chances. It was hard to be sure it was a good one with as slight knowledge as she had of the surrounding terrain, but it was the only one that seemed feasible to her at all. Twice a day, with a group of patients and two attendants, she walked through the grounds. The fence, she felt fairly sure, would not be too great a hazard. Half a mile from Hilltop House, where she was living now, there was a hollow where trees grew thick and close to the fence. On her first walk there she picked out the one that she could get over. She would have to count on doing without a rope of any sort; it would mean a dangerous jump, but she thought she could manage it. The hollow was hidden from the buildings within the grounds, and so far as she could see there was no highway nearby. She'd have to strike out and try to find it for herself, for she wouldn't dare make inquiries. But how to get alone and unattended to the hollow was a more serious problem.

She judged that after a time, if she behaved herself, she would have considerably more freedom to wander about the grounds. But no one would give her an inkling as to how long the time might be, and meanwhile what was happening to Adriana? And how were the sinister designs of the criminal who had brought her here working toward their completion? Doris resolved not to wait if she could find any opportunity to get away from surveillance.

The opportunity came so soon and so unexpectedly that she could not believe at first that it wasn't a trick. Every afternoon she shared organized sports with the other patients from her house. It was a trying hour; the available sports were limited, as no one in Hilltop House was allowed to use any object which could be converted into a weapon of attack. Croquet and hockey were thus automatically eliminated. From among tennis, badminton, volley ball and basketball, Doris chose tennis. She liked the game and played well. But she seldom had a partner or an opponent who played even passably. Worse than their lack of skill was their complete lack of interest. Doris was not quite sure whether it was worse to try to play tennis or bridge with three other people being compelled to go through the motions of a pastime in which they lacked the faintest incentive.

She was plodding through a particularly difficult set, consisting almost entirely of faultless service on her part, when one of the nurses on the sidelines said suddenly:

"You really like to play, don't you, Mrs. Meredith?"

Doris threw her a glance of such comic dismay that she laughed.

"No, I mean in a decent set you'd enjoy it, wouldn't you? I'm going to take you over to the main courts and let you have some fun."

"Thanks," Doris said. "I would like that."

They started together across the green lawn, two young

women in white strolling casually side by side. Doris swung her racket as she walked. A hundred yards from the court, they were stopped in their tracks by a scream so horrible that Doris instinctively covered her ears with her hands. The gesture did not shut out the noise, a terrible, high-pitched but masculine wailing, the sound of a lost soul in torment. They turned and looked back; there was a melee on the volley ball court, and half a dozen attendants were running to the scene.

"Wait here," the nurse said. "No, go on over to the main tennis courts, you know where they are, and say we sent you."

She was running before she had finished the sentence.

Doris stood quite still. She was wearing a white cotton tennis dress and sneakers, with nothing on her head. Fortunately she had on stockings. She had, of course, no purse, no valuables of any sort unless the tennis racket could be exchanged for money. But if she missed this chance, when would another come?

She walked slowly in the direction of the main tennis courts. It would be perhaps an hour before anyone would miss her. If she met anyone before she got to the hollow, she could pretend she had lost her way. If she met anyone in the hollow, after she had started to climb the tree, or if she broke a leg in jumping, it would be the worse for her.

Her heart beat very hard. She made herself walk slowly with her eyes bent on the ground as if in the deepest abstraction. She wanted to look back toward the volley ball court so badly that the desire was like a physical force. The terrible screaming had stopped, to be followed by confused animal sounds. Were they still all concerned? Was anyone watching her? She dared not try to find out. Here was the little clump of trees beyond which she could bear to the left, away from her course and away from observation. She still walked slowly. Whatever happened, however close she came to her destination, she must not run—she must not, she must not.

She turned left and walked a very little faster and with more determination, looking where she was going. If anyone met her, she was looking for the main tennis courts. She still carried the racket. There was no sound of pursuing footsteps. She crossed an open space of lawn where she could see and be seen from the main lodge. She did not look toward it, but she was suddenly oppressed by a fearful certainty that someone was watching her—someone sitting quietly at ease, like a cat with a mouse, ready to let her run as far as her almost exhausted strength could carry her. She would not look, she would not, but the certainty was so strong she almost sat down on the ground and wept for despair. She passed behind a clump of shrubbery and headed for the thicker shelter of the trees. If she could only be beyond the reach of those eyes, nothing else would matter.

Irresistibly compelled forward, she broke into a run. What if she were caught and taken back? At least she must try now that she had her chance. She was gasping as she reached the shelter of the hollow, bent almost double, and there were tears on her cheeks.

She did not stop to look around or reconnoitre; too late for that; it was now or never she must make her break for freedom. If the cat's paw were descending even now in its final, crushing blow, there was yet a chance to dodge.

She climbed nimbly, with all her old skill. She even had a thought to spare for keeping her dress as clean as she could; if she got away she would need to look as clean and respectable as she could manage to work out the next part of her scheme successfully.

There was an exhilaration in climbing; she paused, ten feet from the ground, and looked about her. It was like the Robert Louis Stevenson poem:

> Till I look down on the garden green,
> Down on the roof so brown,
> Up in the air I go flying again,
> Up in the air and down.

The branch that grew over the fence was appallingly fragile—otherwise, of course, it would have been pruned. She must forget her dress now, lying on her stomach, inching along. She wrapped the bandana from her head about her right hand, and held the barbed wire down when the branch sagged against it. Now to swing down, holding by her hands. And now to drop. Too late, too late! The cat's paw had swooped down on its victim. She felt rather than saw a figure at the foot of the tree. She shut her eyes and let go of the branch.

The shock was jarring, but she fell on hands and feet, crouching, and after a moment she felt sure no bones were broken. And there was no one beneath the tree on the other side of the fence. "All a product of a sick fancy."

The trite phrase came unhappily to her mind. Had she left behind her only hope of health and happiness? Too late to think of that now; now she was alone against the world. She must get away from this fence as fast as she could, strike out for the highway, and put her plan into operation.

Chapter 10

DR. OWEN was having a very unpleasant dream. He thought he was in a hospital, but not in his usual role. He was lying in bed, a patient, and a very miserable patient. His head throbbed; he ached all over. His left shoulder and his right hip were worst, but it was hard to choose among the various parts of his anatomy. Miss Pomeroy was in the dream; she was not in uniform, but was sitting beside his bed in a stiff hospital visitor's chair, wearing a brown linen suit. Every time he opened his eyes and turned his head to look at her she said "Good morning, doctor" in a pleasant, professional tone. It was very irritating. He wanted to tell her so, but in the dream he couldn't speak. If he turned his head the throbbing became intolerable. And besides all that there was something he must remember to do, something urgent, a very sick patient he must see at once, or a consultation. Damn it, why couldn't Pomeroy stop saying "Good morning, doctor" in that silly way and remind him of his engagements, as she was supposed to do?

He turned his head, very slowly on account of the throbbing, and opened his eyes. He was trying hard to wake up, but he still thought he saw Pomeroy sitting beside a hospital bed in a brown linen suit.

"Good morning, doctor," she said again, brightly.

"Stop saying that," he muttered.

Pomeroy's smile changed at once from professional to real. "I thought the last few times you opened your eyes that you were coming to," she said.

A strange nurse, properly dressed in uniform, swam into his line of vision, asking in sugary tones: "Is he conscious?"

He waited, holding his breath in his anxiety for Pomeroy's answer.

"I think so," she said.

"No, I'm not," he contradicted. He tried to tell them where he thought he was and how they appeared to him, but the strange nurse stuck a thermometer into his mouth, and he drifted off into another dream.

It was many hours later that he looked again at Pomeroy sitting beside his bed. She was wearing something different, a soft flowered print dress on a gray background, so it must be a different day. No, in a dream it didn't have to be a different day for things to change.

"Good evening, doctor," she said this time.

He held his eyes open and looked at her. "Where am I?" he asked after a little while.

"You're at the Presbyterian Hospital, doctor," she said. "Dr. Curtis Stone is looking after you. You have a concussion, some torn ligaments in the upper dorsal region, a compound fracture of the right femur and numerous bruises. Dr. Stone thinks there are no internal injuries or complications."

He stared at her, comprehension slowly filling his brain. "How long have I been here?" he asked finally.

"This is the fourth day. Thursday. You were hurt on Monday."

"And how much longer will I be?"

"Dr. Stone hasn't said. I can call him now and tell him you're ready to talk."

"No, don't," he said. The effort of shaking his head negatively was so painful that he lay still, feeling cold sweat on his forehead. He must remember not to try that again.

"What happened?" he asked after a little while.

He thought dimly that he knew the answer. He remembered quarrelling with Thomas Granger—good lord, the man must have thrown the safe at him. Was he in jail? But what Miss Pomeroy said surprised him.

"You—fell in front of a subway train," she said, with the slightest possible hesitation before the verb.

Hillis Owen sat up in bed, regardless of his injuries and the plaster cast that kept his right hip motionless. "Fell, hell!" he said. "I was pushed," and dropped back on his pillow in a dead faint.

When he became conscious again it was dark and Miss Pomeroy was not visible. Another strange nurse in uniform was sitting in her place, reading a paper-covered novel. Dr. Owen got a glimpse of a futuristic picture of a severed arm clutching a torn piece of paper, with a gun smoking in the foreground.

"You'll love this case," he said to the nurse.

She put down the book at once and leaned over him soothingly. "Try to sleep, Dr. Owen," she said. "I can give

you another sedative if you like. Dr. Stone said to leave
it up to you."

"No, thanks," he answered, remembering this time not
to shake his head. He lay still, trying to remember. No use
asking this girl; she'd just give him the sedative and go back
to her fictional mystery. He remembered everything now,
right up to the moment of falling. But one point tormented
him. At the time it happened, had he known who pushed
him? He couldn't remember now, and yet it seemed to him
he could recall having the certain knowledge in his mind
as he fell. It was too late now to find a clue, if the police
had not suspected a crime and made an arrest before this.
And what about Mrs. Granger? One thing, if Tom Granger
had pushed him in front of a subway train, he had almost
certainly not gone home and murdered his wife afterwards.
One violent action would have been enough to release his
tension.

"Is Mrs. Thomas Granger all right?" he asked the nurse.

"Perfectly, doctor," she said, so quickly that he knew
she thought he was wandering and was trying to soothe
him. No use saying any more; if the thing had hung fire
for three days it was too late to do anything now. Better
shut his eyes and try to sleep so that he'd be fit to confer
with Pomeroy and Dr. Stone in the morning.

He did sleep, and woke to full consciousness when the
night nurse was relieved at seven in the morning. By the
time Pomeroy arrived, after he had bathed and breakfasted,
he was feeling quite like himself, although still wretchedly
sore and uncomfortable.

Pomeroy's morning greeting recognized his recovery.

"I know you're full of questions, doctor," she said. "Dr. Stone says you're not to talk more than absolutely necessary, so I'll tell you first everything I think you might want to hear, and then you can ask me about what I've left out. Mrs. Meredith's whereabouts are still unknown, but they're on the track. A traffic policeman stopped her going north on the morning she disappeared. She was speeding, but she told him she wasn't in a hurry. She was alone and appeared to be in good spirits. Mr. Fortune called the office to tell you that and to apologize for what he said to you that day at Keene's. He said Keene's had looked you up and found out you were all right." She sniffed slightly. "Keene's are going ahead now trying to trace Mrs. Meredith from the time the policeman saw her. They think that puts New York City out of the question. Mr. Fortune is hoping for more policemen. He says Mrs. Meredith is not a good driver."

She paused, and he felt rather than saw her looking at him with a sort of motherly concern.

"That's all about Mrs. Meredith, I'm afraid," she said. "Now about other things. I've arranged for a competent substitute in the office—for me, that is; no one is trying to do your work, of course. She'll open the mail and let people know you're hors de combat for awhile. I've been here ever since I got word of your accident; I thought that when you regained consciousness you'd probably want to see me." She was silent, as if she had said all there was to say.

"What about the Grangers?" he asked her, after mulling over what she had told him in a brief silence.

"I don't know anything," she answered quickly. "You

hadn't time to tell me about your interview with Mr.
Granger before the—accident."

If Thomas Granger had murdered his wife, or even man-
handled her very severely, it would surely have been in the
papers, unless, of course, he had concealed her body somewhere on his extensive premises. And if Mrs. Granger had
remained unmolested for three days, she was probably safe
enough. Dr. Owen decided to let the matter go.

"So far as I know there's been no progress made toward
finding Miss Wright," Pomeroy went on. "But I've had an
idea about that while I've been sitting here waiting for you
to regain consciousness. If you think you don't need me
here for a day or two, I'd like to follow it up."

"No," he said violently. "There's been far too much of
that kind of thing, Pomeroy. You and I have gone around
sticking our necks out all we're going to. Dick Fortune's
in charge; he says leave the thing to experts, and that's
what we'll have to do."

"Please don't excite yourself, Dr. Owen," she said. "Dr.
Stone won't let me stay here if he finds I'm overstimulat-
ing you."

He nodded without speaking, and after a moment she
went on.

"What I have in mind couldn't possibly be dangerous,
I assure you, doctor. It may be quite wrong, and for that
reason I hate to suggest it to the detectives. But I would
like very much to investigate it myself."

He looked in exasperation at her gentle, stubborn face.

"I give you my word of honor, doctor, about the danger.
And if I find her, I'm sure I can get her story out of her

better than a policeman could."

"No," he said.

"Good-bye now," she answered. "Dr. Stone is on his way in."

Dr. Stone was jovial about his colleague's mishap, but Hillis realized that there was a pretty strong curiosity behind the joviality. His prognosis was cheerful but vague; it seemed pretty certain by this time that there were no internal injuries and that the concussion was not serious. Hillis would be in the cast for six weeks probably.

"But look here, Stone, I can't spend six weeks in a hospital," he said indignantly.

"You're darn lucky you're not spending six centuries in a grave," the other man answered. "What do you expect to happen when you jump in front of a subway train?"

"Is that what they're saying I did?"

"The engineer swears you did. I've got a slew of policemen after me to let you make a statement."

"Send 'em in; I'm ready to make it."

"Make it to me first; I'd like to hear whether it's sensible."

"Somebody pushed me," Hillis said. "I know it sounds screwy, but it's so."

"Any idea who?"

"None I could pass on to a policeman, or even to you."

"You'd better just say 'none' when the police start asking you. Any idea why?"

"A very good one. And that's why I can't possibly spend the next six weeks here in a plaster cast."

"Wait and see," Dr. Stone advised. He scratched his

head. "You'll have to cook up a better story than that before I can let the police at you," he advised. "They'd hound
the life out of you if you started hinting around at mysterious secrets like that. I think I'd better hold them off a
couple of days anyway."

"I don't suppose it's any of my business," he added
after a momentary silence, "but just for curiosity I'd
like to know myself who did it and why."

"The person who did it is going to wind up in the electric
chair," Hillis said. "When he does, I'll tell you all about it."

"You can't kill a man for attempted murder."

"The one I'm after didn't stop at attempted murder."

Dr. Stone whistled softly. "Not a patient then?"

"You've already made me talk five times as much as
you'd let me with Pomeroy. How about running along and
letting me get some of that rest you're always talking
about?"

"O.K. You're the doctor. But I'm going to be around
for six weeks, and don't think you'll have any secrets left
from me by the time they're over."

Dr. Stone went away and Hillis lay still and tried to rest.
But it proved quite impossible. Pomeroy didn't come back;
he was full of things to discuss with her, and he grew more
and more impatient as the hours dragged on. What could
the woman be doing? She said she had a substitute at the
office, and she never seemed to need time for shopping or
facials or visiting relatives or the other distractions of most
females. It was late afternoon before it came to him suddenly that she must have defied his orders. She was out on
the new track that she thought might lead to Miss Wright.

And there was no way to stop her—no way in the world. Betty Wright, Doris herself, and now Pomeroy. The fool. The silly, stubborn, delightful, warm-hearted old fool.

She had sworn to him on her word of honor that there was no danger, and Pomeroy was nobody's fool. But no one could tell on a thing like this. He hadn't expected to be pushed in front of a subway train either, when he went to interview Thomas Granger. He fretted himself into a fever, and when the night nurse came on duty he had to ask her for a sedative. She had gone to get it when Pomeroy came in, walking softly on her rubber shod feet, and smiling the smile of the cat who has eaten the canary.

"Where have you been?" he demanded accusingly.

"I'm sorry, doctor," she said. "I just had to try it."

"So you worried me into a high fever all for nothing?"

"Not quite for nothing. I haven't made any progress on Mrs. Meredith, but I've found Betty Wright."

"You've found her? You mean seen her? Talked to her?"

"I've just come from talking with her."

"But, damn it, she's bound to know something. Those two disappearances one after the other couldn't possibly be coincidence. If you can't get it out of her, turn her over to Keene's. They can."

"I promised her I wouldn't, doctor."

"You promised me you wouldn't go out of here on a wild goose chase."

"Oh, no I didn't, doctor!" she protested, shocked at the accusation. "You ordered me not to, but I never said one single word about whether I would or wouldn't."

The night nurse came back with a hypodermic syringe

neatly arranged on a sterile pad, and looked disapprovingly at Pomeroy. She understood that this was a privileged visitor, but she disliked having her orderly routine disturbed.

"What's that thing?" Pomeroy asked.

"I was worried about you," Hillis answered sullenly, like a small boy caught stealing apples. "Take it away," he said to the night nurse. "I'll be able to sleep now when I'm ready. Fine Watson you turned out to be," he added to Miss Pomeroy when the night nurse was out of sight.

"I always was surprised that Dr. Watson allowed his friend to behave so foolishly," she answered.

"For goodness' sake tell me," he said. "Or is it part of your fun to keep me on tenterhooks?"

She looked at him reproachfully.

"I told you right away that I didn't know anything about Mrs. Meredith," she said. "What I did find out is much more interesting if you will allow me to approach it logically."

"You're right, as always," he said. "Excuse me."

She sat down beside the bed and folded her hands primly.

"What we all need on this case is time to think, doctor," she said. "While I was sitting here beside you, I had a good deal of time on my hands. I got to thinking about all that has happened. We've been running around interviewing people and looking for clues, and we've never stopped and tried to reason things out. I started with Miss Wright because she seemed the easiest problem of all. People don't just walk out of their houses and vanish; they go somewhere and do something, even if it's to be murdered and have their bodies thrown into the ocean. The Keene people have been working on Betty Wright on the theory that she had some criminal connections or intentions, and they haven't gotten anywhere. But she came to the Merediths with good references; Mrs. Meredith is a careful mother, and must have checked those references quite thoroughly. It couldn't do any harm, then, to start on the assumption that Betty was just what she purported to be, and try to work it out from there."

The light glinted on her glasses, and she looked earnestly at the doctor.

"Excellent so far," he said.

"You don't need to interrupt me with comments," she answered coldly. "Just lie still and listen. If I want you to say anything I'll ask questions. Supposing Betty was a respectable young girl who got involved in a mess like the Meredith one through no fault of her own, she'd have been very badly upset by the police questioning and what she'd consider her guilty secret—that she took a drink with her employer when she was on duty. Well, Betty was upset. That fitted. Suppose, then, the cross-questioning kept up until she couldn't stand it any longer, and she made up her mind she had to get away. Where could she go? What could she do? Well, police and detectives go on the theory that people return to their accustomed haunts. It's a sound theory. So the Keenes and you tried to get track of Betty in her home town. You found out that she hadn't gone home. Her father and mother were respectable lower middle-class people, and they didn't seem especially concerned about her. That struck you as just an example of callousness, but it seemed very curious to me. It isn't the way people like that generally react to the disappearance of a daughter.

"Well, Betty didn't go home. What else could she have done? She might have committed suicide, but it's not easy for a suicide to dispose of her own body. She might have been murdered, but all the signs pointed to her having done something of her own accord, and it seems a pretty strong coincidence to expect a murderer to have struck just when she did that. Well, now, doctor, what could a respectable young girl do that would take her away from all her old associations, not worry her parents, conceal her identity, and yet not make her so conspicuous that her new associates would be suspicious of her?"

"Of course," he said. "Put like that it's obvious. But if she had a boy friend how did she ever keep the police and the private detectives off him?"

"She'd only been with the Merediths a week. References give your family background and your previous employers, but they don't say anything about your suitors. And Betty hated it all badly enough that she was anxious to keep him out of it. As a matter of fact she warned him as soon as she was released after that first questioning, and he had sense enough to do what she asked instead of stepping forward and getting himself messed up in it trying to be a knight errant."

"And after I saw her at Meredith's, she called him up and said she was ready to marry him right away."

"That's what she did. It's what I figured she must have

done. So I wanted to go through the marriage licenses issued. Of course I had no way of guessing where they might have done it, and I thought it might take me several days, going through all the five boroughs and nearby points in Jersey and Connecticut. But as it turned out it was right here in Manhattan. The young man is a plumber named Jerry Mahoney. They're very happy. They've moved from the address he gave on the license, but I didn't have any trouble finding their new one. I just picked out the neighbor who seemed most determined not to tell me anything about where they had gone, and explained to her that I wanted to warn Mrs. Mahoney about how to keep away from the people who were on her trail, and the dear old soul broke down at once and told me. I have a face that inspires confidence," Miss Pomeroy concluded smugly.

"You certainly do," Hillis responded with awe.

"So I found the Mahoneys," Miss Pomeroy went on, "and I had very little trouble putting Mrs. Mahoney at her ease. I told her about Adriana's new nursemaid and about poor young Mrs. Meredith, and I promised her faithfully that if she would speak freely to me I would keep her secret and not set the police or private detectives on her trail again. And I hope I am to be allowed to keep that promise, doctor."

"Of course," he said, "of course. But, Pomeroy, they're bound to get her. You're smart, of course, but private detectives aren't dumb. If you thought of it, they'll think of it."

"I doubt it," she said. "It's too obvious. They're so used

to dealing with criminals that they've forgotten how respectable people's minds work. Like the Purloined Letter. When she was sure I wasn't a policewoman or a detective, Mrs. Mahoney talked very freely to me. Things have been preying on her mind. She was fond of Adriana, and felt ashamed of herself for leaving the child like that. She was glad to hear they had a good new nursemaid, because she didn't like Mrs. Meredith senior, and didn't think she was a good person to have charge of the child."

"Didn't, eh? She might have thought of that before she walked out."

"I think she did, doctor. I judge she had a difficult time there, and only stuck it out as long as she did because of the child."

"What's the trouble?"

"Mrs. Meredith sounds psychopathic to me. She was very demonstrative with the child, Mrs. Mahoney said, but wouldn't cooperate in her discipline or any regular scheme of life. She ignored meal hours and nap time, and put her to bed at night just whenever she happened to feel like it. She'd give her candy and toys and hug her and cry over her until she had the child crying too, and was always trying to get her to make extravagant statements about how much they loved each other. And she talked about the parents all the time, and tried to set the child against her mother."

"She ought to make a good witness at the custody hearing."

"I promised not to disturb her, doctor."

"Well, if that's the situation, somebody's got to get the

little girl away. I hope Doris doesn't know all that."

"Mrs. Mahoney says she was always talking about what a good boy and young man Mr. Meredith used to be before he met Mrs. Meredith. She said Mrs. Meredith and her set had led him astray, started him drinking and smoking and keeping fast company, and she's rescued Adriana from people like that and will never let her go back. Mrs. Mahoney says she even talked sometimes as if she'd kill the child before she'd let her mother have her."

Dr. Owen whistled softly.

"Could you take her word for things like that, Pomeroy? She looked a bit hysterical to me herself."

"She doesn't seem so now especially. I tried to allow for some exaggeration, but it sounded bad enough at best."

Dr. Owen tried to remember everything Doris's mother-in-law had said and done during their brief interview. She had seemed an unpleasant old lady, but not, he thought, a dangerous one. But if the girl's testimony were to be believed, she would have to be included in the list of suspects. A woman who would murder her own son to remove him and his child from bad company was not a phenomenon outside a psychiatrist's ken, and yet she should be sufficiently unusual to impress herself on his attention. Mrs. Clifford Meredith hadn't seemed to him in the least interesting. He had merely wanted to get away from her.

She fitted into the physical possibilities of the crime fairly easily. She could certainly have gained access to the Meredith apartment at any time without arousing her son's suspicions. The question of her alibi for the evening had never been raised at all, for she had never been under the remotest shadow of suspicion. If she had been on the subway platform four days ago, she could have pushed hard enough to knock Dr. Owen over the edge. But could she by any possibility have lured Doris away from home? She didn't seem clever. She had the child, of course, to use as bait. But how could she have persuaded Doris to say that she was going to help him, Dr. Owen? If Doris had made any sort of appointment with her mother-in-law she would have had no reason for not telling her own family.

It was the same thing all over again. His mind went around and around in senseless circles. He sighed.

"Try and check Mrs. Meredith's alibi for the night of the murder, will you, Pomeroy?" he asked. "The records of the trial may give you all you need to know. If she could by any possibility have been on the scene, check up on where she was last Monday afternoon too."

"Yes, doctor," she said, making notes. "Now, about Mrs. Meredith. Mrs. Mahoney was very much concerned to hear about her disappearance. She says she is a kind and considerate employer and a good mother; she really seems fond of her. But she hasn't the faintest notion where she could have gone."

"Can't you sit down and reason that out too?" he asked bitterly.

"Mrs. Meredith is a more complex character, doctor. And there is the suggestion of another person's complicity."

"Yes, of course," he said impatiently, and then, with difficulty: "Did Mrs. Mahoney think there was any possibility she might have been—wandering mentally?"

"No, she didn't, Dr. Owen, and neither do I."
Hillis sighed and tried to shift his position in the bed.
"You're a good soul, Pomeroy," he said.

Chapter 11

THE next morning Dr. Stone allowed the "slew of police-men" represented by one mannerly and intelligent detec-tive lieutenant to interview his patient. Hillis found the ordeal both more and less difficult than he had anticipated. The lieutenant accepted his statement that he had been pushed without any evidence of incredulity, but his ques-tions thereafter bore uncomfortably close to the point.

"You're quite certain it couldn't have been an accident, Dr. Owen?"

"As certain as it's humanly possible to be."

"And yet you have no idea who could have pushed you? I'm not asking you to swear out a warrant for anyone's arrest, you know; I only want something to go on."

Hillis shook his head slowly, noting with pleasure that the process was definitely less painful than it had been. "I didn't see a thing," he said. "What about the engineer? He must have seen it all."

"He says you jumped," the lieutenant offered cheer-fully.

"Yes, I know. So Dr. Stone told me," Hillis said. "How do you decide whom to believe?"

"We've been checking up on you and haven't found any motive for suicide or any indications of suicidal intention, so we're inclined to believe you."

"Thanks."

"Not at all. But I'd be obliged if you could be more helpful. How could you feel so certain you were pushed intentionally without having any idea who did it?"

"There's a feeling to an intentional push," Hillis said. "It's hard to describe—but I believe anybody'd know. In a crowd like that you're sort of braced for being accidentally brushed against. I was pushed hard and suddenly; it caught me off guard."

"Let's go at it the other way, then. Who would be likely to want to kill you?"

"I'm a psychiatrist, you know. I deal with a number of unusual people. My treatment must arouse resentment in some of them, and I don't always know which ones."

"How about naming a few likely ones?"

Hillis shook his head again. "You can't set the police trailing neurotics on suspicion. It would undo all my work."

"O.K., doctor." The lieutenant stood up, still pleasantly. "If you want to leave a potential killer wandering around loose rather than risk losing a paying patient it's your funeral—and I only hope that won't turn out to be literal."

The man was trying to make him so angry that he would blurt out a name, and he almost succeeded. If his suspicion were only a little less absurd, Hillis thought, or if he had even one fact to base it on, he'd risk naming a name. He hoped they wouldn't start now to shadow all his patients.

That would be a fine how-de-do. He'd told the literal truth throughout, without saying anything that might lead them to connect what had happened to him with the Meredith case. He wondered whether they knew he had been talking to Thomas Granger just before it happened. The police didn't bother presidents of New York department stores unless they had something pretty definite to go on, he supposed.

The lieutenant was standing looking at him as if he could read every thought through a small glass pane in his head. That was how his patients must feel about him, Hillis thought. He had a sudden impulse to tell the lieutenant the whole story. Wouldn't it be the best thing for Doris? But after all, it really wasn't his business—or was it? If it were merely a question of finding her, he would certainly put the police onto it. With their facilities they were far better equipped than he or the Fortunes or any private agency. But it was a question of finding her without alarming the desperate creature in whose power she must be. Hillis turned his head away and closed his eyes to remind the lieutenant that he was ill and easily tired.

It was the middle of the following week before he was allowed any other visitors. Dick Fortune was the first. He came in looking apologetic and carrying a florist's box. Hillis was appalled to see how the strain was telling on him. He was haggard; he had lost weight, and his skin was pasty. Unwillingly Hillis felt himself softening toward the man.

"I'm not much good at apologies," he began.

"Skip it," Hillis advised. "You had a perfectly good point. As a matter of fact I still haven't justified myself for butting in."

"Doris never told me you were a psychiatrist," Dick said. "Would it be asking too much to inquire whether she consulted you professionally?"

"I'm afraid it would," the doctor said. "I couldn't tell you if she had without her consent. Matter of ethics. You can consider that saying yes or no, just as you prefer."

"It's more pertinent than it sounds," Dick explained. "We've got track of her through a private mental hospital up beyond Utica. She's been there as a patient the whole time. But yesterday she escaped."

"The hell you say!" Hillis looked at him, thunderstruck. "What's the name of the place?"

"Glenview Lodge."

"It's o.k. I know it. But how did they ever come to take her as a patient without communicating with the family?"

"They thought I knew about it. She was supposed to be there for observation. They said she arranged it herself, but they had some letters with my name signed too. The last one said I was going to be away for a month, and would call for a report when I got back. But when she got away they tried to find me at once, and of course I was right here in my office."

"Who paid the bills?"

"They say they had a check with my name signed to it. Matter of fact, they still seem to think I fixed it and that I'm reneging now for private reasons. Of course I'll honor the check if you can vouch for the establishment—they took good care of the poor girl. The reason I asked about her consulting you—they said she wanted them to get in touch with you. They tried to, but they just got a letter back from your office saying you were ill and couldn't be disturbed."

"Oh, lord!" he groaned. The efficient substitute Pomeroy had found. Pomeroy had never seen the letter. Hell's bells, it must have been there the Monday he was hurt. He remembered Glenview Lodge on one of the envelopes that were all too obviously only business. But why hadn't Pomeroy opened it after he left to see Thomas Granger? Too late to worry about that now. It was enough that she hadn't.

"That alters things, of course," he said. "Yes, your sister consulted me. She was troubled by bad dreams and insomnia after the trial. I'm afraid I wasn't much help to her, but I was able to assure her she was quite normal."

A spasm of pain contracted Dick's features. "Poor kid," he said huskily.

"That brings up a question I've wanted to ask you," the doctor said. "Did you know that your great grandfather—same name as yours—had died insane?"

Dick stared at him blankly. "No," he said. "Did Doris tell you that?"

"No, she didn't. I'm puzzled to know why not. It was in some genealogical papers she left for me to look over." Hillis didn't think it necessary to strain the recently renewed amity by mentioning just how he had secured the papers.

Dick shook his head again, looking puzzled. "No, I

never knew that. I wonder how Doris found out. It's serious, isn't it? I mean for Adriana, and my children if I should ever have any."

"No, it isn't. Insanity that far back, if it hasn't recurred, is negligible. But it must have preyed on Doris's mind to make her keep it secret like that."

"What in heaven's name has been going on in Doris's mind?" Dick burst out. "And what can she be doing now? Why should she have run away from the place instead of communicating with me if she wanted out?"

"Dick, I'm going to offer unasked advice once again," the doctor said. "Get the police now. There's no more reason not to. Nobody knows where Doris is, but we're working against a fiendishly clever mind. We need all the help we can get on our side. Ask the police to help us find her before her husband's murderer does."

"I don't see that at all," Dick said. "All her husband's murderer wants is to be let alone."

"That's where you're wrong. Whoever it is is after Doris too. I don't altogether see why, but I'm perfectly sure of the fact, and I'm beginning to have some dim suspicion as to who's involved. We can't afford to take another chance with her, Dick; when we find her she'll need protection. I beg you to get the police."

Dick looked stubborn and reserved, and Hillis went on desperately: "I know what you're thinking. I've been wrong on every count so far. If I'd been attending to business instead of running around like a chicken with its head cut off, I'd have read the letter that would have told us where Doris was ten days ago, and I wouldn't have wound up in the hospital either. Go ahead and say it; it's all true, but just the same, this time I'm sure I'm right, and I beg you to call the police now."

"If I do, it kills Doris's chance to get custody of Adriana. I don't get this set-up at all, doctor; I don't understand what Doris was doing in that place; I don't know why she went to you. If I appealed to the police for help, they'd ask a lot of questions I couldn't answer. There'd be no chance in the world of avoiding publicity; I can't subject Doris to all that."

"You're willing to risk her life against a little more unfavorable publicity?"

"How do I know I'm risking her life? It sounds a lot more as if it's her sanity that's at stake, and I want to go easy."

Hillis abandoned the argument, unconvinced but hopeless. "Are you going up to Glenview Lodge to pick up the trail or sending one of Keene's men?" he asked.

"Both," Dick said. "I'll want to talk with them myself, of course. They sound completely baffled, though. They're sure she had no money and no clothes but what she was wearing. They say it's not too unusual for a patient to get away, but they're always picked up within a few hours. They were so sure of that they didn't try to get in touch with me until she'd been gone twenty-four hours, and they haven't found a trace."

"I wish I could go with you," Hillis said. "Ask them to write me a full report on their findings while she was there, will you?"

"Yes, I will," the lawyer answered, rising. "And from

now on we're working together." He made it half a statement, half a question.

"For Doris's good," Hillis said, and then, abruptly: "I suppose you know I love her."

"I suppose I do," Dick agreed, "and I suppose I resent it. It's unwholesome, I know, between brother and sister, but that's the way it is. I never liked Jerome Meredith very well."

"Don't go around magnifying it by fancying it's unwholesome," the psychiatrist advised. "People hardly ever like their in-laws. It's nature. Have you any real objections to me as a suitor for Doris?"

"If you say Doris is fit to marry again I'm profoundly grateful to you. But I hope your emotions aren't swaying your judgment."

"Forget it," Hillis advised. "Your sister is all right."

When Dick was gone he lay back on his pillow and hoped it was true. Scarcely three weeks ago it had been only a game. The amateur Sherlock Holmes would solve a six-months old murder without taking any time away from his profession. And now here he lay, chained to a hospital bed while the woman he loved was in mortal danger. Damn it, he wasn't licked yet. He still had his brain, and whatever else he lacked he had all the time he needed to think. Somehow, somewhere, in the facts he had now at his disposal, he must find the clue. He'd have Pomeroy bring the papers from the Meredith apartment and he'd go over those again. And lying here alone at night he'd sift the people and the motives, one by one. He had an even

chance now to save Doris, except that the murderer would
be able to look over the scene of her escape for clues, and
he couldn't. If Dick Fortune wouldn't call the police, it
was up to Hillis Owen to save Doris. No one else could do
it; no one else appreciated the terrible peril. He must find
her first. He must. He must.

The next afternoon his nurse came in, looking troubled.

"There's a Miss Scott out here to see you. She isn't on
the list of visitors Dr. Stone approved, but she says she's
come in from Westchester on purpose to see you, and I
hate to turn her away."

"Aunt Fanny," he said. "Let her in, of course. Dr. Stone
just didn't think of her coming."

It was a funny thing at that. He'd never met Miss Scott
but twice in his life, and she hadn't shown any particular
fondness for him either time. She was probably one of
those old ladies who take a ghoulish pleasure in visiting the
disabled. He folded his hands on his breast and smiled
wanly in preparation for her.

The old girl ought to be in the hospital herself, he
thought when he saw her. They were all taking this thing
hard; of course it must be a terrific strain after the tragedy
and the trial.

"This is awfully good of you, Miss Scott," Dr. Owen said,
feeling as he spoke that the remark was entirely inappro-
priate.

"I hope it's not presuming to trouble you now," she
said. "I wouldn't want to send your fever up or anything
like that, but of course a broken leg isn't exactly like an

illness, is it, you have to be quiet but your mind is active, and with all the time you have on your hands it seemed to me it might be presuming less this way than it would to come to your office when you were well, but if you don't want to listen, just say so and I will go away."

"Of course I want to listen, Miss Scott," he said gently. "Is it about Doris?"

"About Doris? Well, yes and no; that is, it certainly concerns Doris, and she is wound up in it from beginning to end, but on the other hand it's not exactly about Doris. Oh, I see what you mean; is it anything new about Doris? Well, no it isn't, but perhaps after I tell you what I want to tell you, you'll know how to find her."

"Please begin at the beginning then, Miss Scott, and let me get it all straight."

"That would be going much too far back. And there's a lot of it I wouldn't want to discuss with anyone outside the family; all that really matters to a stranger, Dr. Owen, not that you're a stranger, but still I wouldn't want to tell you all the family secrets, is that I shot Jerome Meredith."

She leaned back in her chair with a little sigh of relief, and sat regarding the doctor with an air of childish trust and confidence. It was as if, having told him her secret, it had become his problem and she had nothing more to worry about.

He lay very still and regarded her. "Why are you telling me this?" he asked at last, gently.

"Because I don't know what to do and I don't know who else to ask. I couldn't tell sister or Dick; they'd feel so dreadful, and I didn't see how I could go up to a policeman who was a perfect stranger and tell him, and, well, it just seemed to me you were the best person."

"Why did you do it?"

"It was the way he was treating Doris. I only meant to talk to him, and I went there that night I knew Doris would be away with Dick, and there he was with that dreadful Granger woman, and I simply couldn't endure discussing it; I just shot him."

"Where did you get the gun?"

"In Doris's room. It was his too. He let me in; he was just as pleasant and polite as he could be. I thought we could have a good talk; it wasn't the kind of thing I'd like to discuss with a young man, but still Doris is my niece, and almost like a daughter to me, and I was willing to do it for her sake, and thought everything was going to go along nicely and perhaps I could make him see the error of his ways, and then I saw that—that dreadful woman, and I said I'd go to Doris's room to leave my coat and hat and powder my nose, and I must have opened his bureau instead of Doris's—I didn't know my way around very well, I hate New York and apartments—why people should want to live like that I'm sure I don't know; rabbit warrens. So I opened this drawer full of men's things, and there was the gun, and I thought 'I'll shoot him,' and so I did."

"But Mrs. Granger must have seen you."

"Certainly she saw me."

"But she swore she was at home on Long Island all that evening."

"She swore to a lie."

"But, Miss Scott, if you did all this for Doris how could

you let her stand trial for the crime?"

"Dick was defending her; I knew she would be all right."

"And if she hadn't been?"

"I could always have confessed afterwards, after it was all over. But I thought when she was acquitted it would be finished; we'd have nothing more to worry about, and they've kept on and it's just gotten worse and worse until I'm desperate; I can't stand any more. I was going to kill myself, Dr. Owen, and leave a note explaining how it was, and then I thought perhaps that wouldn't be necessary; Doris going to that place really gave me this idea; if they thought I was crazy it wouldn't seem so dreadful to them, would it? Could you say I was crazy, doctor, and it wasn't really my fault, or do you think I'd still better kill myself?"

She spoke as casually as if she were asking him to choose between two hats, but he didn't make the mistake of answering her casually.

"Don't do that," he said. "If you really care at all for any of them, don't do that, Miss Scott. Nothing could be worse, from every point of view. In the first place, if you were to kill yourself and leave a suicide note, the police would think it was phony. They'd tear down the house out there looking for more clues, they'd be so sure that Jerome Meredith's murderer had killed you too, and forged the note in an attempt to leave a clean slate. Nothing in the world would convince them that you were a murderer and a suicide; you aren't the type, Miss Scott. Don't, I beg of you, kill yourself in the belief that it will end this case; it won't."

"What shall I do then?"

"I'm not certain," he said. "I need to think about it a little. Mrs. Granger's out as a witness, isn't she? She's too much involved in perjury to dare to testify against you. But why did she try to get money from Doris if she knew you did it? And who lured Doris away and where is she? And why?"

"I don't know." Aunt Fanny began to cry. "I started it, and now it's way beyond me, and I don't understand it at all any more."

"And who pushed me off a subway platform, and why? You aren't lying, are you, Miss Scott?"

"Why ever should I say I did it if I didn't?"

"Lots of reasons. Too many."

He lay still again, and there was no sound in the room but the noise of her sobbing. The nurse came in, and at sight of the tableau looked alarmed.

"Now, now, now," she said, "we can't have visitors upsetting our patients like this."

"Run along, will you, Miss Glenn?" he said. "This is serious. I'll wind it up as quickly as I can if it bothers you."

She hesitated, looking concerned and indecisive.

"Run along," he said more sharply, "I'll take the responsibility if Dr. Stone has any objections."

"Ten more minutes, then," she said. "I couldn't let her stay any longer, Dr. Owen, without calling Dr. Stone."

"All right, all right," he said. "We'll finish in ten minutes."

Miss Glenn left, looking worried, and Hillis thought it

highly probable that she would, on second thought, curtail his ten minutes, or at best listen at the door to the rest of the conversation. Nevertheless there was nothing for it but plain speaking; they had been beating about the bush too long already.

"The thing for you to do, Miss Scott," he said, "is to make your confession to the police. Never mind their being strangers; go to headquarters and tell them you have some information about a homicide; they'll steer you to the proper man and you can tell him the whole thing."

"Oh, no," she said, drying her eyes. "I couldn't possibly do that. That's just why I came to you, so I wouldn't have to."

"Miss Scott," he said, suddenly losing patience, "this is a murder, not a musical comedy. I am immeasurably shocked by the frivolous attitude your whole family is assuming in the matter. Surely a woman of your age and experience knows that you can't shoot a man, confess to a casual acquaintance, shed a few tears, and be done with it. If you want to confess, you must confess properly and to the proper authorities. After that, if there's anything I can do for you in my professional capacity, I shall be very glad to. At present you're asking me to compound a felony."

"I shouldn't want to do that, doctor."

"I'll be quite frank with you, Miss Scott. I don't believe you. I don't think Mrs. Granger saw Jerome Meredith shot; if she did her conduct since the trial has been absolutely inexplicable. I don't think you could shoot a man in cold blood. I'm almost certain you couldn't let Doris go through the trial as she did without telling the truth at least to her, if you had done it. I'm telling you to go to the police as a sort of challenge. 'Put up or shut up' it might be phrased in less genteel circles."

"I—I don't know what you mean," she whimpered.

"Oh, yes you do. If you didn't kill Mr. Meredith, there's only one reason for claiming you did. That is because you think you know who did, and you want to shield that person. But look what you're doing instead. You're immeasurably limiting the field of possibilities; it practically narrows down to your sister, your nephew and your niece. Do you think one of those three did it? Do you know one of those three did it?"

"I tell you I did it," she sobbed. "You're cruel. I did, I did, I did."

"Nobody but Sidney Carton ever got away with that," he told her. "It simply doesn't work. Believe me, it always does more harm than good. But look here now, Miss Scott, if you can't convince me, an amateur criminologist lying here in a hospital bed, what hope have you of convincing anyone in a suicide note? It won't wash, I tell you, and you'd better not try it."

"All right," she sobbed. "I'll tell you the truth, and then you'll see why I can't go to a policeman with it. It's my fault even if I didn't do it; it's the penalty for my sin, and much, much more terrible than I ever dreamed. Doris isn't my niece, Dr. Owen, she's my daughter."

"Your daughter! But what about Richard? They're twins."

"They were born the same week: that was how sister

could conceal my disgrace."

"You mean Doris is illegitimate?" Miss Scott nodded her head, sobbing audibly.

"Who was her father?"

"It was 1914. He was—I suppose he was an adventurer. He seemed so gallant and brave. He went to Canada and enlisted before he knew about Doris, and he was killed in action before she was born. He would have married me if he'd known and if he could."

"Does Doris know this?"

"No, neither of them has ever suspected. Sister's husband didn't want to do it, at first, but she won him round, and he grew to be as fond of Doris as he was of Richard before he died."

"But how could you deceive people?"

"None of sister's friends knew me well. I was living alone in New York, studying art, and she was out in Westchester, so I went west to Ohio to have my baby. I was supposed to be a widow, and sister went to a hospital in New York and wouldn't have visitors and stayed until I was well enough to come back. And then she took both babies home and said they were twins, and I went along to help her."

She was telling the truth, Hillis thought with a sinking heart. And he had only seconds to cross-question her before Miss Glenn's inexorable return.

"You think Doris did it?" he asked her.

"I tell you I did it for Doris's sake," she sobbed.

"Miss Scott, you don't have time to lie now. You're going to have to go out on the street in a minute; Miss Glenn is just ready to chase you out of here. You don't want to make a public spectacle of yourself. Pull yourself together now."

"If Doris did it, it's because she's having to pay for my sin, and I can't endure that. I want to suffer for her."

"If Doris did it and you do what you're contemplating, you'll burden her conscience with the suicide of her mother as well as the murder of her husband."

Miss Glenn was as good as her word, and came back in reproachfully:

"I can't tell you about any other visitors that aren't on your approved list now, Dr. Owen," she said. "You shouldn't have let her come in if you knew she was likely to go to pieces like that."

"I didn't know it," he said. "I'll talk to Stone tomorrow; I'm going to have to have more visitors instead of fewer. Never mind; it really hasn't hurt me, Miss Glenn."

He lay back and tried to think. So that was it. Aunt Fanny only thought Doris was guilty, of course; she couldn't be sure. But, good lord, if what she said was true, Doris was no relation to Richard Fortune, d. insane 1847. It fit better one way but worse another.

What was Aunt Fanny covering up? Was she smart enough for a double finesse? Had she really done it herself, and did she hope now to cover her tracks by making an absurdly improbable "confession"? He pondered for a long time. Then he made two telephone calls. The first was to Miss Pomeroy.

"Listen," he said. "I have another job for you since you're so good at vital statistics. I want you to look up the birth certificates of Richard and Doris Fortune in Manhattan in August 1915. And after that go down to the Lost Property department at police headquarters." He gave her careful instructions. "And keep quiet about this," he concluded. "I mean really quiet."

"Yes, doctor," she said, "but I don't understand what it means."

"Never mind," he said. "You'll be safer if you don't know. And if it's there you'll find it."

He hung up, and then, with the telephone on his chest, meditated the space of one cigarette before he dialled another number.

"This is Dr. Hillis Owen," he said, "calling from the Presbyterian Hospital. I'd like to speak to the detective who interviewed me last Saturday morning regarding my accident in the Forty-Second Street subway station. I want to add to my statement."

Chapter 12

RUTH GRANGER wakened with a start, the sense of terrible oppression that hung over her returning instantly and completely. She was not really free from it even in sleep, but waking was worse. She opened her eyelids wide enough to survey the room without allowing anyone who might be in it to notice that she was awake. The room was silent and empty; the early summer sunshine made a cheerful pattern on the sea-green carpet, and from outside there came faintly the gay voices of early morning bathers in the

Sound. She shivered and reached for a filmy negligee of rose satin and lace to wrap around her shoulders.

Then, delicately, with an expression of horror and aversion, she reached under her pillow and touched the frayed edge of a bit of paper. The look of loathing on her face deepened, and she drew it out. It was a single sheet of cheap notepaper, soiled from handling, and with paste smeared over it. A newspaper clipping was pasted to it.

NOTED DOCTOR IN SUBWAY ACCIDENT. Her eyes ran again, with a horrid fascination, over the brief account of the accident to Dr. Hillis Owen. The words below the clipping were printed in red crayon. WHEN YOUR TURN COMES I WON'T MISS. It was just as it had been; nothing had changed; nothing had happened to her. As if following an impulse stronger than her own will, she looked quickly under the bed, and then opened the doors of her closets. She hesitated a moment before pushing back the rows of dresses to look at what might be behind. Nothing. The room was just as it had always been, last night, yesterday morning, the morning before that, back to the dimly remembered days before the note had come.

But this was unendurable. Death itself couldn't be so bad as this going constantly in the fear of death. This sort of thing couldn't happen in America. It was what police forces were for. She looked at the white enamelled french telephone beside her bed. All she would have to do would be pick it up and dial police headquarters—they had a technique for dealing with threatening letters. But was it a technique that could do her any good? What was the use of having the author arrested if she were lying somewhere with her head bashed in—a bloody mess like Jerome Meredith's—she mustn't think like that. Another day to get through somehow, and today she must do more than make the hours pass; she must think of a plan, talk to Tom, somehow get away from this terror. Tom had loved her once; surely he would help if he knew she went in danger of her life. Surely he would help unless the threat came from him. She shivered again, and went into the bathroom, subjecting the shower stall to a brief examination, and carefully locking the door behind her. She stepped carefully too, to avoid slipping as she bathed and dressed. Most of the murders that escaped detection, people said, were made to look like accidents. There were so many ways an accident could happen at home and no one be the wiser. If Jerome Meredith's death had looked like an accident it would have been forgotten long before this. Jerome Meredith's blood and brains spattered all over his favorite leather chair. No. No. No. She mustn't start the day like this.

She dressed and went downstairs for breakfast. She had been accustomed to have the meal in her room, but no one knew what might happen to a tray on its way to a bedroom. If she were in the dining room with Tom—but it was foolish to fight it like this. She must decide, one way or the other. If Tom hated her enough to do that, there was no escape, living in the house with him. A dozen times a day —a hundred times a day—he had the opportunity he needed. If it were Tom, she must get away or tell the police. But how could she go to the police; how could she answer their questions? If they would just find out for her who had written the note, and then leave her alone—but the police didn't work like that.

The table was laid for breakfast in the sunroom. The two glasses of orange juice stood ready in their nests of ice. Ruth looked quickly about the room, and changed the glasses before she sat down. Tom must have seen her do it; he came in almost at once, and glanced curiously at her as he sat down without a greeting. He did not touch his orange juice. She sipped in silence and watched him as he rang for eggs and bacon and coffee.

He looked up from his paper and met her eye; there was a curious expression at the back of his: hatred, fear, irresolution?

"Do you want to go to Reno?" he asked her abruptly.

She was instantly wary, looking for the trick.

"Not particularly," she said. "Do you want me to?"

He patted his mouth with his napkin. "I understood you were bent on going," he said drily. "Isn't there someplace we can go and talk without the servants continually popping in and out?"

"The servants know everything we do and say anyway; why try to cheat them now?"

"I thought perhaps you'd rather not have what I want to say overheard."

"I'll take my chances. Leave the pot," she said to the maid who came in with the coffee, "and don't come in again unless we ring, please." She felt for the buzzer with her toe, to be certain she could reach it quickly.

"I'm ready to give you the money to go to Reno whenever you like," he said when the girl was gone. "This hasn't been very pleasant for either of us. I'm prepared to take care of all your expenses and pay twenty-five hundred a year alimony until you remarry. If you ask for more I'll fight it."

"Can I live on that?"

"Not on this scale, but you won't starve."

She looked at the untouched glass of orange juice.

"Why are you doing this now?"

"I'm not enjoying my—revenge as much as I expected to. And anyway we couldn't go on like this forever."

"And how about Doris Meredith? Do you still think I have her concealed in a closet somewhere about the premises?"

"I don't know anything about it," he said, "but it doesn't seem funny to me. We'll skip the kidding, if you'd just as soon."

"I'd just as soon."

"We can't talk like this," he said impatiently. "Drive into town with me; we can be alone in the car and in my office."

"No," she answered. The monosyllable was both breathless and defiant, neither of which she had intended. He looked at her in surprise.

"Why not, for heaven's sake? Are you determined to do nothing I want? It only complicates arrangements."

"We can talk here," she repeated stubbornly.

"Not the way I want to talk."

"Anything you can't say here it would be better not to say."

"Will you give me one good reason for not doing as I

ask?" he inquired patiently.

"I'm afraid." Her tone was still defiant.

"You're afraid," he said with astonishment. "By God, that's good. You're afraid of me. Why don't you shoot me then? Put me out of the way for good and all?"

"Don't," she said, her voice rising. "Don't, don't, don't."

"You're right," he said. "There's no sense in that. It's over; we have to go on somehow. You say you don't know anything about Mrs. Meredith; I have to take your word for it, for I have no way of proving the contrary. I've told her brother you don't; as far as I'm concerned that's the end of that. We can get back to our own affairs."

"Listen, Tom," she interrupted. "What can I say to make you believe that I was lying to Doris Meredith about that night? I didn't see anything; I didn't hear anything; I swear it. I went to the door and found I couldn't get in, and that was all. I was frightened; I pounded at first, and then—"

"And what can I say to make you believe that I don't want to know any more about that night?" He was shouting now. "I don't care to hear how you and your paramour passed the time, nor about your misunderstandings. I know where you were and I know why you were there; I know a lot more than I want to know about it, and I won't hear any more."

"Tom, please. I know you have reason enough for not believing me—"

He laughed bitterly.

"Tom, did you send me a threatening letter?"

It was out now. Now she would know.

"Did I what?"

"I had an anonymous letter threatening me. Was it from you?"

He laughed again, shortly. "I can still talk."

How could you be married for ten years to someone and know him as little as she knew Tom? He was as mysterious to her as any casual stranger on the street—his thoughts, his feelings, his plans.

"Listen, Tom," she said. "Please. I know things have happened that can't be mended with words. But, believe me, last year when Jerome was alive, I didn't know you cared what I did. I thought—"

"Quiet!" he roared. "I will not listen to that muck."

She was silent, and after a moment he spoke again, more calmly. "You wanted to go to Reno so badly that you brought yourself low enough to ask that woman for money. You risked reopening the case and branding yourself a perjurer and worse—"

"Not worse. What do you mean?"

He flung an Anglo-Saxon monosyllable at her, and watched the patches of angry red stand out on her cheeks as if he had struck her.

"You wanted the money that badly," he said, "and now you don't care whether or not you go to Reno. May I ask you to explain that?"

"I want to do what you want me to do. I'm sorry for what's happened. I want to make it up to you."

He laughed again. "How are you going to make it up to Jerome Meredith?"

Jerome Meredith with blood and brains spattered over his favorite chair. The picture came back again unbidden, and would not go away. That was what Tom wanted. It was what he meant for her too. If not today, tomorrow, and if not tomorrow, next week. Reno would be only a respite —or was he going to do it in Reno? Was he preparing an alibi? And what would it be—an accident on the train, a lethal poison introduced into a harmless bottle of aspirin, a disappearance in the west? Perhaps he would send her out on the train and fly after her himself. Blood, and Jerome Meredith in the chair where she had so often seen him, leaning his head back, laughing. She couldn't stand this much longer. But of course that was just what Tom wanted. He was trying to make her do it herself so there would be no guilt, no trial, no clues to trace.

"You're trying to make me kill myself," she said thickly. "I won't do it, I tell you; I won't; if you want to be rid of me you'll have to murder me, and if you murder me you'll die for it."

"Hush," he said. "You're hysterical; you'll have the whole household here. Be quiet."

He seized her shoulders and tried to shake her, but she twisted away.

"Don't touch me," she screamed. "You murderer."

Mrs. Clifford Meredith was dressing her granddaughter Adriana for a shopping expedition. She brushed the child's curls with loving attention to detail, tied and retied the blue hairribbon and picked almost invisible bits of lint off the little coat and hat. The little girl stood patiently under her ministrations, but her eyes were large and anxious.

"Just like your father," her grandmother crooned. "He was always such a good little boy; he stood still to let me dress him just like you. He was a pretty little boy, too, like you; it's like brushing his curls all over again to handle yours; it brings it all back to me."

"Boys don't have curls," Adriana said.

"Your father did. Little boys used to wear them longer than they do nowadays, you know. When he was a big boy and they had to be cut off I cried and cried; your grandfather thought I would be sick; I slept with one of your father's curls under my pillow for ten years. I still have it put away in a little box; I'll show it to you."

"Don't cry now, grandmother," Adriana said. "I'm a girl; my curls won't have to be cut off ever."

"They're beautiful," the old woman said, "but yet not so beautiful as your father's were." Her voice quivered, and the anxiety in the child's expression deepened.

"I wish we were going to see my mother today," she said.

"You can't forget her, can you?" the old woman answered. "No matter how much I do for you, it's always your mother you want. Will you remember me like that when you're gone from me?"

"Yes, grandmother," the little girl said, politely and obediently.

"That's what you say now, but you want to go off and leave your old grandmother; you don't care what becomes of me; you can't wait to get back to someone that doesn't love me." The old woman was weeping openly now, letting the tears run down her cheeks and making no attempt to brush them away.

"My mother never cries," Adriana said.

"A woman who never cries is a heartless wretch. I won't talk against your mother, Adriana, now that you're too young to understand, but some day you will know what I've done for you and which really loves you better, your mother or your poor old grandmother."

"I love you, grandmother." The child began to cry. "I love you, I do."

"Not the way I love you. It's too much to expect of a child; it's only natural; you're young; you don't understand what's happened; of course you're loyal to your mother; I don't hold it against you."

"I love you the most," the little girl said.

"That's my girl." The grandmother brightened up, brushed her tears away, and set about making herself ready. "That's the way your father used to talk to me when he was a little boy. No little boy ever loved his mother more than he did. Oh, Adriana, if I could only keep you a little child forever! If your father could only have stayed a sweet little innocent child such as you are now! Nobody knows what a mother suffers when her children grow up and love someone else more than they do her."

"Does my mother suffer?"

"I don't know, I'm sure. I'm not one to turn a child against her mother; far be it from me to say anything against her, but when you're older you'll understand that there are special reasons why you stayed with me instead of with your mother. You're happy with me, aren't you, darling? We do such lovely things together. You love your old grandmother, don't you? I love you more than anything else in the world, and I want you with me so much I'd do anything to keep you—anything. I've done things already you could hardly believe just so you could be my little girl and stay with me and never want to leave me for anyone else."

The child and the grandmother were both crying, locked in each other's arms, when the younger Mrs. Clifford Meredith came into the room.

"Oh, mother!" she said. "You've got her all wrought up again. You promised you wouldn't."

"Have I said anything, Adriana?" The old woman appealed to the child. "Haven't we just been talking pleasantly about how much we love each other and about your father? Can't a grandmother talk to her grandchild about its own father—her own son? Things have come to a pretty pass if I don't dare mention the name of my son because his wife might not like it."

"Mother!" the younger woman said. "You know Clifford told you when you let the new nursemaid go you'd have to be awfully careful if you wanted to keep her. Come on, Adriana," she said to the child, "let's get your doll."

"I'm going down town with grandmother."

"Later. You don't want to go down town with your eyes all red from crying. Come on and get your doll now, there's a good girl."

"I love you best, grandmother." The little girl flung her arms around the old woman's neck, and clung to her with a torrent of tears.

"There, what did I tell you?" The grandmother was triumphant. "She loves me. She doesn't mind telling me so. Am I a bad grandmother, pet? Do I get my baby all upset? Did I say anything to you at all except just to tell you how much I love you? Is that a wicked thing now, a grandmother can't tell a child she loves it?"

Jane Meredith picked up the little girl, and carried her into her own room grimly. She took off the small coat and hat and set the child down in a little cushioned rocker. "Play with your dolly now like a good girl," she said. Adriana was sobbing as Jane went back to her mother-in-law.

"Mother, you'll have to stop that if you want custody of the child," she said. "She's only a baby; it's not good for her to be kept stirred up like that all the time, and if the judge knows it he won't let you keep her."

"I only told her I loved her."

"But talking like that all the time, and hinting things about her mother and her father—well, see for yourself what it does to her."

"I never say a word against her mother. I'm very particular not to."

"I can't see why Doris hasn't tried to see her these last three weeks." Jane frowned. "It looks to me as if they have something up their sleeves they're going to spring for a surprise. Honestly, mother, don't you think it would be better to let her go? She's a dreadful burden for a woman your age."

"Never. I'll never let her go. She's my life. I'll take her away before I'll let them take her away from me. We'll hide; we'll go off where no one can find us. I've been through too much now ever to let her go back."

"What do you mean, mother, always saying things like that? It worries Clifford. You don't know how bad it sounds."

"You don't know anything, any of you. You don't know what it is to be a mother, Jane, how can you know what it is to lose a son?"

"We do know, mother, we all felt for you."

"I don't mean when he died. I lost him before that. When he started following that woman, when he thought of her before he thought of his mother and what he'd always been taught, when he began doing bad things, nobody'll ever know what I suffered. And now I have her for a comfort, and I'll never give her up to anybody, no never. I'll do something desperate first."

Miss Pomeroy was just finishing her report to Dr. Owen.

"There were none reported lost or stolen," she said, "but there was one found unclaimed at that place the next week. Would that do any good?"

"Of course," he said. "Of course. Much better."

"I don't know what you're talking about," she said, "and I don't understand about the certificate either. Why should anyone steal a birth certificate? There might be some uses for a copy, but why steal the original? It must have been terribly hard to do."

"It wasn't stolen, Pomeroy," he said. "It was never there. Don't wonder about it. I know I sound like an egregious ass, but I have a reason. I should never have sent you on that job; forget now that I did. Forget what you found out, and don't try to figure out what it means. As soon as it's safe I'll tell you. This is serious; I can't put that too strongly."

"Dr. Watson again," she said smiling, but there was no answering smile on his face.

"Don't give me anything else to blame myself for," he said. "Forget it."

"Certainly, doctor," she said. "But may I ask first—has it been any help to you?"

"I see the light," he said, "but the lord knows what I ought to do now. If I could only get to Doris—"

"But you have the police after her now."

"Yes, I've done that much. They can go over the ground and pick up her trail if there is one. But if the wrong person gets to her first—". His voice broke with the easy emotion of illness. Miss Pomeroy frowned anxiously.

"It's worse than a nightmare," he said, "lying here like this, thinking of all the possibilities, trying to decide what to do, realizing that everything I try may be the wrong thing."

"You mustn't worry," she said. "Now you've told the police everything they can go ahead. That's what you've thought all along that you ought to do."

"But I haven't done it," he said. "I told them about Doris, where we had the last trace of her, and how she disappeared. And I told them that I thought I must have been pushed by someone who was afraid of what I was finding out or had found out about the Meredith murder. But I didn't say anything about Mrs. Mahoney or the Grangers."

"You left out the Grangers?"

He nodded miserably. "That's just the way I feel about it. But somehow I couldn't mess in that again. Look at it my way, Pomeroy. I went to her husband, carrying tales about his wife, making trouble, because I thought it might help us find Doris. It didn't. If I hadn't done that, I might have felt I could sic the police on Mrs. Granger. But if I do I've got to tell them she committed perjury; they'll go in there and rake up an old, painful story. I couldn't carry tales in the family and to the police. It was just a bit too much of the Meddlesome Matty even for me."

"But the whole case turns on her story," she said thoughtfully. "If we knew she was telling the truth when she said she didn't go into the apartment that night, we'd know certainly that Mrs. Meredith was innocent."

"Sure we would. Can the police find out which time she was telling the truth, though? If they scared her into a maze of more complicated lies, we'd be worse off than ever. It seems to me the only chance of getting her to tell the truth is to win her good will and keep her from being scared."

"That's supposing she didn't do it herself."

"I know, I know," he said. "Every single decision I've had to make on this thing has carried a heavy penalty for someone if I guessed wrong. If one of the Grangers did it, I've made the worse blunder of all now. But, you know, Pomeroy, I don't think either of them did. More than that, I've got a sneaking hunch they're fond of each other underneath all this."

"Sometimes, doctor, I think you're an incurable sentimentalist," she said.

"Sometimes I think I am," he admitted. "Moreover, we've got to face it, there's one thing about the Grangers that smells awfully queer. I'm assuming that someone pushed me in front of a train because of what I might find out about this murder. But Mrs. Granger has openly hinted that she saw or heard whoever did it. Why wasn't she a candidate for murder before I was?"

"Maybe the murderer had no chance to get at her. Mr. Granger's scheme kept her pretty close at home."

"Maybe. And maybe she did it, and maybe he did it. How do detectives keep from going crazy?"

"The police are handling it now, Dr. Owen, and you'll have to rest," she said. "Worrying can't help Mrs. Meredith."

"I know," he said. "There's one thing I'd like to do for her, Pomeroy, but it means making you the goat again."

"What is it?"

"I'd like to get that child away from her grandmother. I can get Judge Ryan to come in here and see me about it, and I think my opinion carries enough weight with him to induce him to take her away if I say it's best. But I don't believe she'd be any better off with the Fortunes while things are the way they are now. I wondered if you—" his voice trailed off.

"You mean you'd let me have her? Oh, doctor, I'd be delighted."

"You're a good soul, Pomeroy. I'll see if I can fix it up."

"But you can't give me any hint of who it is you suspect?"

"No fooling, Pomeroy, I can't. It still doesn't make
sense, but that's not what's important; it's dangerous, too.
I can tell you this though; I'd give my right arm to find
Doris before the other person who's after her does."

Chapter 13

WALKING the twenty miles to Utica would, Doris expected,
be by far the most difficult part of her escape. Jumping
over the fence with its barbed wire guarded top was nothing in comparison. She did not dare risk hitch-hiking any
part of the distance, and a twenty-mile walk in tennis shoes
was stiff sport.

It was late afternoon when she made her escape, and
there would be no use in arriving in the city late at night;
she must sleep somewhere along the way, and yet she must
arrive in Utica looking at least tidy enough to avoid being
conspicuous on the streets. She kept the tennis racket for
what protection it might offer against tramps and stray
dogs, although she knew it would help to mark her if a
search had started. She located the highway without much
difficulty, and after orienting herself on it she started to
walk eastward, paralleling the road but keeping herself
out of sight.

She set a fast but not gruelling pace; she wanted to put
as much distance as possible between herself and Glen-

view Lodge before nightfall, but she must, at all costs, look like an ambitious hiker and not a hunted fugitive. The success of her scheme for escape exhilarated her, and she walked along easily, enjoying the panorama of summer landscape. It was good to be free, to be young, to feel the warm blood pounding in her veins. For a little while she could even forget her anxiety about Adriana and about herself. She wanted to walk as far as possible the first day; hunger would plague her the next morning, she knew, but she dared not ask for food. She had no map and could not ask for one, but she remembered the road quite clearly from the time she had first traversed it, scarcely two weeks earlier. She found a few blackberries to eat, and after dark she discovered a deserted shed where she ventured to lie down. She didn't sleep as if she had been in her own bed at home, but she woke at early dawn refreshed and pleased to find that excitement was still stimulating her so that the long walk ahead of her and what she must do in Utica did not frighten her too badly.

She would have liked a cup of coffee, but she made a drink of well water do instead, stifling unwelcome thoughts of possible typhoid germs. Beggars couldn't be choosers, and this would be the hardest day of all. It was noon when she reached Utica, hot, dusty and footsore. She felt as if everyone she passed on the street must be staring at her, but when she dared look at anyone she met, it was generally to find him passing her quite incuriously. She abandoned the tennis racket as she approached town, and walked through the streets, a red-faced and perspiring young woman in a somewhat soiled and creased white sports dress, her damp hair clinging to her bare forehead.

She headed for the center of town, and as she approached it she began to watch for a solid and substantial looking church. Her heart was beating uncomfortably fast; this was the most difficult part of all. She must have her wits about her now, and play her part properly. She passed two churches that looked as if they would do, and forced herself to turn into the third; looking farther was merely cowardly, an excuse for putting off an unpleasant moment. It was a big, gray stone church, nondescript as to architecture and not too new. She paused in the vestibule and looked over the notices. The pastor's name was listed—the Reverend Mr. Carl Fowler. That would make it easier. There was an unlocked washroom off the vestibule, and she went in and made herself as presentable as she could. Her heart sank at the sight that met her eyes in the little black-framed mirror, but washing her face and hands cooled her, and she brushed back the hair from her forehead and sat down for a few minutes to collect herself and be sure she had her story straight.

She knocked at the door of Mr. Fowler's study, and a voice called: "Come in." She pushed the door open and walked into a book-lined room, sparsely and somewhat shabbily furnished. A gentle, graying man looked inquiringly at her from his chair on the far side of a wide oak desk. He had steady, kind blue eyes. She took a deep breath and plunged into her story.

"Mr. Fowler, I'm in trouble. I haven't any claim on you, but I thought perhaps—"

"Come in and sit down and tell me about it," he said. "Miss?"

"I can't tell you my name," she said. "When you've heard my story you'll understand why."

He nodded gravely and gestured toward a battered leather chair beside the desk. She sat down. This wasn't going to be as hard as she had supposed. She had picked her church well; it would have been dreadful if instead of Mr. Fowler she had encountered one of the bright, up-and-coming, modern young ministers.

"I came to Utica to be married," she said. "I live in a little town I'd rather not mention, just as I'd rather not tell you my name. My—my fiance was—is—a travelling salesman. He's been coming to our town for quite a long time—more than a year. We've been engaged for six months. My parents never liked him very well. They didn't forbid our marriage, but they hoped I'd change my mind. That was why he persuaded me to come here to be married. He thought—he said that when we went back home married it would be easy for them to be reconciled. We came here together yesterday; when we got into town it was too late to get a license. But we went to a hotel together anyway, and he registered as my husband."

She felt the color flaming in her cheeks convincingly as she told the sordid, commonplace little story. Mr. Fowler sat regarding her gravely, attentively, with no change of expression.

"This morning we went to the City Hall again for a license," she said. "He left me there on the steps. I waited two hours. When I telephoned the hotel, I found he had checked out."

She stopped breathlessly. She had told it all right! She was on the verge of tears herself, tears of pity for the poor, silly little country girl who had been betrayed and deserted.

"What is his name?" Mr. Fowler asked.

She shook her head. "I don't want to tell you that either."

"And which is the hotel where you were registered?"

"I'm sorry," she said. "I can't tell you that either. I'm asking your help, but I'm asking you to take me on trust."

"What do you want me to do?"

"I need money—enough to get home. Twenty-five dollars would do."

He did not answer yes or no. "You have no hat," he commented.

"I can't go back to the hotel," she explained. "Not for anything. I can't face the clerk."

"You want me to give you twenty-five dollars so you can go home? But what will you do there? Your parents and neighbors will know you left to be married."

"My parents will take me back in spite of what's happened. Perhaps they can keep the neighbors from knowing."

He looked at her gravely and kindly.

"You're not telling me the truth," he said. It was a simple statement of fact; there was no condemnation in his voice.

"What makes you think that?" There were tears in her

eyes; she blinked them back angrily. "You want me to name the hotel and the man," she said. "You want me to pillory myself—"

"No," he said. "I want you to tell me the truth."

"You won't help me?"

"Not unless you'll tell me the truth."

She stood up dramatically. "Then there's nothing for me but the streets," she said. It was like a line from a nineteenth century problem play, but she delivered it with feeling. He was standing too, regarding her gravely.

"I should like to take you home with me to lunch," he said. "Perhaps if you were to talk with my wife it would be easier for you to tell her what is really troubling you."

"I won't tell your wife any more than I've told you," she said stubbornly, although the thought of food made her feel faint. "I'd die of the shame—I'd rather die, or go on the streets. I thought your work was to help people."

"It's not that I won't," he said gently but inflexibly. "I can't help you until I know the truth."

"I need twenty-five dollars," she said. "That's the truth."

"Let's have lunch," he suggested.

She went with him in sullen silence, sitting beside him in the shabby sedan without a word as he drove into the residential section of town and stopped before a shabby, comfortable, dark green frame house. Mrs. Fowler was a plump, cheerful lady, and neither she nor the minister's two sons, boys of ten and twelve, seemed to find anything remarkable in the unexpected appearance of a strange, hatless and very hungry lady for lunch. As she ate home-made vegetable soup and oatmeal muffins with a relish she could not disguise, Doris found herself speculating on what sort of a household this must be that could accept her so unquestioningly. The Fowlers were both more worldly and less conventional than she would have expected them to be. She still couldn't see how Mr. Fowler could be so certain that her story wasn't true. She had tested it over and over in her own mind; it should certainly have convinced a kind, unworldly man like this preacher.

After lunch, at their father's suggestion, the boys cleared the table and went out to play baseball so that their parents might converse uninterrupted with the guest.

"This young lady is stranded in Utica," Mr. Fowler said to his wife. "She's in trouble that she doesn't feel free to tell me about. I think perhaps if the two of you can talk it over together we can get somewhere."

He stood up at his place, ready to leave the room.

"No, don't go," Doris said. "There's nothing I could tell Mrs. Fowler that I can't tell you. It's just—you're right—I can't tell you. I thought ministers were kind and good; I thought you'd help me because I needed help. Forgive me, I shouldn't talk like this. I'm grateful for the lunch, but I must go away now, and I don't know what's to become of me."

"If I gave money to everyone who came to my office asking for it," he said, "or even to everyone I thought really needed it—I wouldn't have any left to live on. But I am concerned about you. I wish I could help you. I'm certain I could if you would tell me the truth."

"Oh, no, you wouldn't," she said bitterly, and then suddenly: "If I tell you the truth, will you lend me the money?"

"Yes," he said soberly. "I think I can promise that. Yes."

"But you won't," she said. "It's a trick to find out, but when you do you'll go back on me. I don't blame you. Anybody would. I would myself."

"I give you my word," he said.

"All right," she answered, bitterly, recklessly. "I escaped yesterday from a private mental sanitarium near Wampsville."

She made no addition to the bare statement, but sat staring cynically at the man who had promised to help. He stared at her, gravely, calculatingly, and then nodded his head.

"Yes," he said. "That's true."

From the corner of her eye Doris saw Mrs. Fowler's frightened face, and that she opened her mouth to speak. Her husband made a slight, imperious gesture, and she was silent.

"You want money to get home?" he asked.

Doris shook her head. "I can't go home just yet. There are things I don't understand about why I was sent there. I need a little time alone to get things straightened out in my mind, to make some inquiries. I wanted your money to get a presentable outfit and rent a room somewhere so I could get a job. I was going to pay you back."

"What kind of job?"

"Stenographer, I suppose. Or clerk in a store. I haven't

ever worked, but I can type a little."

"But do you suppose you could get work like that without a reference or any background?"

"I don't know. I've never tried. I think so, though. With proper clothes I'm quite presentable, and I'm educated and have nice manners."

"My dear child!" he said. "And you thought I was unworldly!"

"I can't go to my friends," she explained, "because I don't know who are my friends. I know that sounds as if I belong in the sanitarium, but nevertheless it's true."

"If we let you stay here," he asked, "would you communicate with your family and let them know you are safe and well?"

"Yes," she said. "But I couldn't impose on you like that." She looked full at Mrs. Fowler's frightened face.

"We keep no maid," he said. "The work is heavy for my wife. If you were to stay, you could share it; you would not need to be under obligation. You could stay here indefinitely as a general maid without causing any comment."

"But—but—wouldn't you be afraid?" she stammered.

"If we find that we have assumed too heavy a responsibility for your safety we may, in time, have to return you to your friends," he said. "But we wouldn't do that without telling you first."

Doris looked at her hostess.

"Are you willing, Mrs. Fowler?"

"Of course," she answered. "Willing and glad."

"You're very good," Doris said. "I'll let you see the

letter I write my brother, but not the address, if you please."

"That won't be necessary," he assured her. "There's a bedroom in the attic, and Mrs. Fowler can find you a few clothes to tide you over for the present. I'm glad you came to us, Miss—"

"Call me Doris Scott," she said. "Doris is my first name. And Mr. Fowler—someday, somehow, I'll repay you for this kindness."

She wrote the letter to Dick that afternoon in the attic bedroom, chewing on the eraser of her pencil between sentences. It was a difficult letter to write.

Dear Dick:

I'm safe and well here in Utica, and you mustn't worry about me. I've been—or did you know?—at Glenview Lodge, near Wampsville, a mental sanitarium. Dick, did you send me there? Please don't equivocate. I'm all at sea —and it means so much to know. If not you, will you see if it was Dr. Owen?

She tore that up and tried again.

Dear Dick:

I hope you haven't been worrying about me. I'm well, safe and happy, but I don't think I'd better come home just yet. I'll explain when I see you—it's all pretty complicated. Meanwhile, will you write me here, General Delivery, and tell me how Adriana is, the status of the custody case, and whether you have found out anything new about

Jerome's death? Don't scold me, Dick; I'm not being mysterious just to be annoying. I don't know who to trust—
hardly even you, darling. Love to mother and Aunt Fanny,
and try to keep them from being too upset.

As ever
Doris

P.S. Have you seen anything more of Dr. Owen?

It wasn't much better, but she let it go. You didn't need
elaborate explanations with Dick. Perhaps she was foolish to do this, instead of going to him, but in this fantastic world where there was no solid ground underfoot,
nothing to hold on to, it was hard to be certain even Dick
was to be trusted. She pressed her hands to her aching forehead and wondered again if she should have stayed at Glenview Lodge and let them try to help her.

The days that followed at the Fowlers did help. Doris
had had no idea of the amount of physical labor involved
in running a house. How did Martha do it at home, and
never seem hurried or tired? Doris made beds, swept,
dusted, mopped, scrubbed, went marketing, prepared
vegetables, cooked, washed dishes, set tables, mended for
the lively little boys, ran errands, and dropped onto her
cot at night so tired that she was asleep before she could
worry herself into insomnia.

Dick's reply to her letter, which came almost at once,
was upsetting, but she had little time to brood over it.

Dear Doris, he wrote,
What in heaven's name are you doing? You've had us

all nearly frantic. We didn't know where you were at all until last week after you left Glenview Lodge, when Dr. Grant there communicated with me. Why did you go there in the first place, and, having gone, why on earth did you leave in that insane fashion? And what is this wild talk about not being able to trust your own family? I will do what I can to calm mother and Aunt Fanny down, but I don't understand it, my dear girl, and I don't like it. Please write me at once and let me know where I can talk to you. There's nothing new on Adriana; I don't really feel that I can go ahead until I understand a little better just how things stand in regard to you.

                                    Your loving brother,
                                            Dick.

It wasn't like Dick's loyalty and understanding, but she had put a terrific strain on both during this past year. No mention of Jerome or the murder investigation, not a word about Dr. Owen. Doris was not willing to admit to herself how much she longed for some explanation of Dr. Owen's conduct. Had he sent her to Glenview? If he'd only done it straightforwardly, she would have been willing to stay.

She wrote Dick again, but still guardedly. She couldn't hint at any suspicion of Aunt Fanny in a letter to Dick. If he could only write her that the case had been solved—that it had been Ruth Granger or her husband, or some burglar, or even poor Betty Wright. And yet, if she wanted to untangle the threads, oughtn't she to get back home and get to work on it? Sometimes she thought she ought to talk the whole problem over with Mr. Fowler, but it was so fantastic, so tangled and so horrible to bring into that peaceful home that she kept silence. Neither Mr. nor Mrs. Fowler asked her anything more about her affairs; she knew they observed her silently, but they seemed satisfied with her conduct and made no comment. She wondered sometimes what Mr. Fowler would say if he knew that she had been tried for the murder of her husband only a few months previously. If only she could be sure it was no worse!

Her second letter to Dick was not answered so promptly as her first. She called three times at the General Delivery window before the day when the clerk in charge handed her a long, white envelope. She slit it eagerly with her forefinger, and as she did so a hand grasped her arm roughly. She drew in her breath in a sharp gasp and turned around; it was Dick, and for a moment she thought she would faint from relief.

"Oh, Dick," she said. "You frightened me. I thought you were—whoever it is I'm hiding from."

"Doris, what in God's name are you talking about?" he asked. He was thin and haggard; there were heavy shadows under his eyes, and Doris felt a sudden, bitter self-reproach at having brought him to this.

"Dick, I'm afraid," she said. "Somebody tricked me into going to Glenview Lodge; I don't understand who or why, but I'm afraid. That's why I'm hiding, and I thought it would be easier and safer to stay hidden if none of you knew where I was, really. But, oh, Dick, I'm sorry. I didn't know it would worry you so."

"That's water under the bridge," he said. "Forget it, Doris, if you're all right." He looked hard at her, a frown of concentration in his eyes.

"You look well," he said wonderingly.

"I have a job," she assured him. "I'm taking care of myself. I'm all right, Dick. You'd better go home and leave me here until you know who killed Jerome."

"Stop talking nonsense, Doris," he said. "Don't you realize by now that we'll never know who killed Jerome?"

"But you wanted me to let you try to find out."

"That was a month ago. We can't talk here in a public place. Where are you working?"

"I don't want to tell you, Dick."

"Where are you living, then?"

"That either. Please, Dick, let me alone just a little longer."

"But I can't, Doris. I can't stall off the hearing about Adriana much longer, and I can't go into court and admit I don't know where you are or what you're doing or why you aren't at home. I can't leave you alone like this."

"You mean you think I'm not responsible? You think I did it, Dick? Was it you that sent me to Glenview?"

"Doris, please, we can't talk about all this in the post-office. I have a car out here; come on now and drive home with me."

"I can't, Dick. I'd have to see the people where I'm staying. They've been kind to me; I couldn't run away without any explanation."

"How did you find a place? How did you manage about money? Until your letter came we expected every day to hear that your body'd been found somewhere. I don't see how you could treat us so, Doris."

"I'll explain it later. Dick, tell me this now, though. Was it Dr. Owen that sent me to Glenview Lodge? Does he think there's something wrong with me?"

"I haven't talked to Owen. Have you been a patient of his?"

"Yes. I thought you knew."

"I asked him but he wouldn't tell me."

"They wrote him about me from Glenview Lodge, or said they did, and he never answered. That's what I couldn't understand. Do you know why that was, Dick?"

"Please, Doris, we can't talk here."

"Tonight then," she said. "I must get back now. I'll meet you in the lobby of one of the movies—let's see—no."

"We'd better not be seen together if you really mean to go on with this crazy plan of hiding here," he warned.

"I know a place down by the river," she said, and gave him directions as to how to get there.

"How will you get there?" he asked. "You haven't a car, have you? How do you know the place?" His voice was sharp with suspicion.

"I'm not being kept, if that's what you mean," she laughed. "I took two little boys there for a picnic last week; that's how I know the place."

"Can you come alone? Is it safe?"

"I can take care of myself now, Dick. I'm grown up. Perhaps I'll let you take me home. I'm not sure what I ought to do."

"Don't tell anyone you're meeting me," he said. "I've

got a case adjourned because I'm supposed to be sick in bed."

"I won't give you away." She smiled wanly. "It's good to see you, Dick."

"Take care of yourself," he said. "I'll see you at nine tonight or I'll tear this town apart to find you."

"I promise I'll be there. Don't follow me now, Dick. You know I keep my word."

"I promise too," he said, pressing her hand.

Getting out tonight without any explanation wasn't going to be easy, she realized on the way back to the Fowlers'. She had never until now tried to go out in the evening, and they might think it unwise to let her. They still didn't know anything about her.

The truth, she decided, after her single experience at trying to lie to Mr. Fowler, would be her best explanation.

"My brother has found me, Mr. Fowler," she said at lunch. "I gave him General Delivery here as an address, and he came and watched for me in the post-office until I went in this morning. He wants me to go home."

"That seems like very sensible advice," Mr. Fowler said.

"Yes, I suppose you're right," she said. "I've been afraid they'd try to send me back, and it didn't seem as if I could stand it, but I can't go on like this."

"I'll be very glad to talk with your brother and tell him about our experience with you here, if that will be any help to him in making up his mind."

"Yes, of course," she said. "That would be the sensible thing to do. But when I saw him I didn't want to tell him my address. I—well, I'm afraid I've already arranged to meet him down by the river."

Her cheeks burned as Mr. Fowler observed her with his level, measuring gaze.

"Very well," he said at last. "I'll be glad to drive you there."

"Oh, I couldn't trouble you. I'll be quite all right; he'll bring me home. He—it really is my brother, Mr. Fowler."

"I'm sure of that," he said, "but I think I had better take you to the place of meeting."

"He may not like it. He asked if I'd be alone."

"I shan't intrude, but I will take you to the place of meeting."

Doris abandoned the unequal argument. There were a strength of purpose and a strength of character in this gentle little gray man that she had learned to respect.

"I expect I'll decide to go home with Dick, Mr. Fowler," she said, as they drove through the summer twilight to the place of rendezvous. "I can't tell you how much I appreciate all your kindness—and how much he will. I want to tell him about you, and have you meet each other. I've never known anyone quite like you."

"We'll be sorry to lose you," he said. "You've been a good companion."

He parked the car at the side of the road and Doris climbed out.

"Thank you for letting me go down alone," she said. She turned and held out her hand.

"If you should need me, call," he said, clasping it warmly.

"Dick will be here," she said confidently. "I won't need

anyone else." She clambered down the bank to the picnic spot she remembered. She had lost her bearings a little; it was farther than she had thought. She was out of sight of Mr. Fowler's car when she saw the headlights of another parked on the grassy flat. It might not be Dick, she thought suddenly. This was a perfect place for lovers on a summer night, probably the last place in the world to find the privacy she desired. The moon was not yet risen; it was quite dark and the lighted headlights blinded her. She stumbled forward in the bright light; at least she wouldn't slip up on anyone unawares. There was a rustling in the bushes beside her.

"Dick," she said. There was no answer. She stepped out of the headlight beam and called again: "Dick."

Something struck her head a stunning blow. She staggered and reached out, feeling warm flesh. "Dick," she said. "Mr. Fowler." She couldn't be sure whether she was screaming or whispering. Her voice sounded thick and strange. Something seized her and carried her; she fought with all her strength, and then suddenly her hands recognized the familiar body.

"Dick," she murmured. "Dick, it's you."

And the black, choking water of the river engulfed her.

Chapter 14

"You knew it all the time." Doris Meredith stood at the foot of a hospital cot, her hands clutching the foot rail, her dark eyes staring accusingly from her white face. "You knew it and you let me go ahead. You let me be the onc to trap him."

"Mrs. Meredith!" Miss Pomeroy interrupted. "Your brother tried to murder both of you. Dr. Owen has saved your life."

He made a little gesture with his free hand, begging Miss Pomeroy to be silent.

"I suppose you expected me to be grateful," Doris went on bitterly. "I suppose you think I wanted to save my life at the expense of his. Oh, I know"—she spoke now to the other woman—"it was his life or Dick's. A man has a right to defend himself. But to let me betray him"—she dropped her face into her hands.

"I didn't know, Doris," the doctor said gently, "if that's any consolation to you. I suspected, of course; I'd hardly have come into the investigation without some suspicion that there was something in it that brought it into my field. I'm not quite such an interfering fool as I've sometimes looked. It seemed to me there was evidence of a diseased mind at work, and I suspected whose it was. But I had no proof until last week. And I was never certain until then that my suspicion was correct."

"And then you used me as a decoy."

"I did nothing of the sort," he said, speaking more sharply. "I make allowance for your grief, Doris, but please remember I've been under a strain too. When I felt reasonably certain of the criminal, I told the police my suspicions, and the facts on which I based them. They put a watch on your—cousin, and followed him to Utica. If I had had

anything whatever to say about the matter, he would have
been arrested when he approached you in the post-office.
But they felt that the case against him was rather weak
and it might be a good idea to let him incriminate himself further. If you'd been killed in the process, I suppose
someone would have received a reprimand."

"You mean the police were following him last night at
the river?"

"Yes, of course. How else did you suppose you were
rescued?"

"I thought it was Mr. Fowler. I'd promised Dick to
come alone, and then my employer, the man who was
helping me, insisted on coming along to protect me. I
thought he'd caught Dick and called the police all because
I didn't keep my word."

"Then you can set your mind at rest. It was I who arranged to have him seized. How long have you known
that he's not your brother?"

"He told me just before I went to Glenview Lodge.
We agreed for Aunt Fanny's—for my mother's sake, and
for Adriana's, to continue to keep the secret."

"And which of you did he say is Miss Scott's child?"

"Why, I am, of course."

"No, but you're not. He probably told you the same
story she told me, and it's wrong in several important par-
ticulars. I wish you'd sit down, Doris," he interrupted
himself.

Miss Pomeroy pushed a chair forward, and Doris
stumbled unwillingly into it.

"You ought to be in bed yourself," he said. "You have no business here. Let Pomeroy give you a sedative and get you a room here."

She shook her head. "I want to know it all—now. Not knowing has done too much harm. I can't wait any longer."

Miss Pomeroy nodded at him across her head, and he went on.

"In the first place," he said, "you are the legitimate daughter of Joseph Fortune and Margaret Scott Fortune. Your birth certificate is recorded properly—and Richard's isn't. In the first feverish months of the first World War, your aunt fell in love. Early in 1915 she went to your parents and told them she was going to bear a child."

"An illegitimate child," she said.

He shook his head. "That was what she told your mother and father," he said, "but the truth was worse. The man had married her. It was after the marriage that she learned of the strain of insanity in his family, direct, inescapable, handed from father to son."

"No, no, no," she said. "It's fantastic. It's impossible."

"It's true," he said, "and it will help you to feel more kindly toward Dick, who is the victim of a series of dreadful wrongs committed before he was born."

"Dick," she said. "Poor, poor Dick." She put her head down on the counterpane. Dr. Owen wanted to touch the dark hair so close to his hand.

"Your aunt did not tell your parents that she was married to the father of her child, nor what she had found out about him. And your mother thought that coincidence had supplied a perfect solution for your aunt's dilemma. Together they persuaded your father, against his will and judgment, to take Miss Scott's child along with his own, and rear them as twins. The births were expected to occur the same month; they were, as a matter of fact, the same week. Miss Scott's child was a son. She alone knew of his inheritance; she alone suspected when his hereditary insanity began to develop. She was willing to sacrifice you for him, but don't be too bitter about that. She wanted to give her own life for Richard's too, but she realized at last that she couldn't do it; he was too dangerous a man to leave at large. He would never have stopped killing."

"I wish you'd let him kill me," Doris said. "Then he would have stopped. I wish I'd never seen you, and he would have stopped with Jerome. He only went on because he was forced into it."

"I don't think he was trying to kill you," the doctor answered. "We'll never be certain, of course, but I think his plot against you was more subtle and diabolical than that. You didn't see what hit you, did you? And you were semi-conscious when you went into the water; you're a good swimmer, and you were close to shore. I think it was one more step in his scheme to drive you mad."

She stared at him dazedly.

"It's dreadful," he said. "It's fantastic. But if you insist on talking about it today, I insist on telling it truly. There has been too much falsehood for the sake of shielding people's feelings."

"Forgive me," she said. "I know you don't mean to be cruel. I want to hear it all."

"Your father found out the truth about Richard's heritage when you children were adolescent. It was a terrible discovery; by that time he was as fond of the boy as if he had been his own son. But for your sake he planned to tell the truth, and to arrange for close medical supervision for Dick. He put it off too long."

"You mean the money trouble came along and pushed it all out of his mind?"

The doctor shook his head. "Nothing could have pushed that out of his mind. He was trying to decide how he could do it in the way that would be kindest and easiest for all of you, when Dick found out. You say you love him, Doris; you're sorry for him now, but I ask your sympathy for that adolescent boy, high strung, impressionable, sensitive, with all the troubles of the ordinary adolescent plus his bad heredity, when that terrible knowledge came to him."

Doris was staring at him; her hand had crept to her throat. He nodded gravely.

"I think so. It can't ever be proved now, unless he chooses to confess, but I think, like you, that in the ensuing emotional storm he killed your father. He made it look like suicide. He was never suspected; he thought he had come off scot free, but actually he had pushed himself into the terrible abyss on the brink of which he had been teetering. There was a time when he might have been saved from himself, Doris, but that time passed thirteen years ago. You needn't reproach yourself now."

"But how—"

"I don't know or care. You recognize Dick's ingenuity as well as I do. It must have been fairly simple; your father would have been entirely unsuspecting, and the medicine that killed him was a very common one."

"But Dick was fourteen."

"I told you it was a horrible tragedy. I have as much sympathy for Dick as you have, perhaps more, for I know a little more of the darkness of the paths into which his mind has carried him."

Doris sat still, clasping and unclasping her hands. "And Aunt Fanny?" she asked at last.

"I don't believe she suspected until years later. I didn't press her too hard on that point; she's gone through a good deal, Doris."

"But still," Doris said, "even if all that's true, there's still Jerome? Why Jerome? And how?"

"I don't want to go into a technical lecture on the working of a diseased mind. The important thing to remember is this: he loves you, Doris. You'll be able to do a good deal to help him in the years ahead if you can only remember that. He was annoyed at the way your husband was treating you—not a strong enough motive for murder, of course, in a normal man. But once the idea entered his head, it combined with other ideas. He had committed murder before, remember, when he was only a child, and had never been suspected. If it didn't sound as if I meant to be facetious, I might say that he had found he had a talent for murder. He loved you, but he was obsessed with the idea that he was mad and you were sane, when it could as easily have been the other way—or so it seemed to him. It would have been so much better if the boy had been the legitimate child, the one with a sound heritage and a safe future. The idea tormented him until it began to seem to him that he could change destiny. If only you were insane, then, by some strange magic he would be well again —or at least you were with him, still his twin sister in disaster. I can't make it altogether clear because it is irrational. It isn't as cruel, though, as it sounds. In a way it's a perverted form of love. He wanted you with him, and at the same time he hoped to make your sanity a sacrifice for his.

He paused, dejected. "Do I make it a hopeless muddle?"

"No," she said. "I think I see what you mean."

"He deliberately planned to kill Jerome in such a way that you would be suspected, and he hoped in time to be able to make you doubtful of your own innocence—as he did."

"But it was physically impossible."

"I know. That baffled me. I was morally certain he had done it for quite a long time before I could imagine *how*. Put yourself in his place. It was a difficult problem. You had to discover the crime, and under such circumstances that you might possibly have committed it yourself. He had to have a perfect alibi, for he was a possible suspect. Jerome signed his death warrant, I think, when he told Richard about his scheme for getting the nursemaid out of the way at such times as he wanted to entertain Mrs. Granger alone at your apartment. It was bad taste, of course, to his wife's brother. I suppose he wanted to taunt Richard."

"Yes," she said. "He never liked Dick. He'd think it was funny to make him a confidant about his amours— one man about town to another."

"Dick must have seen then the opportunity that gave him. I dare say he expected to kill your husband and Mrs. Granger together, which would have made it look more than ever like your crime. But by a fluke of luck he reached the apartment before she did."

"But he couldn't have known that I'd go home between the acts. I didn't know it myself."

"Certainly not. As a matter of fact that was the most disastrous thing that happened to his plan. He wanted it to appear that you had murdered Jerome *after* coming home from the theater. He planned for you to discover the murder, as you did, and to be alone in the apartment with the body—bodies if things had gone right—the child and the drugged nursemaid long enough to unsettle your nerves thoroughly and to arouse the suspicion of the police. He did three unusual things that night—met you in the lobby instead of coming up to the apartment, left you again in the lobby, and drove to Westchester instead of to his own apartment. He judged shrewdly that you wouldn't call the police until you had succeeded in reaching him, and he knew that would make them suspicious of you."

"I can't believe that," she said. "The rest, perhaps, but not that."

"We're not discussing the actions of a sane man," he said. "He wanted it perfectly clear that he had not been in the apartment during the evening at any time, so that he could have had no part in doping the nursemaid or any of the rest of it."

"Yes, I see."

"He thought that committing the murder between the acts of a play would give him the well-known perfect alibi. He would have the testimony of any number of witnesses that he had been at the theater throughout the three acts. And while it is not impossibly far from the theater to your apartment, the idea of dashing out and back during an intermission is one that would simply not occur to people. He felt very sure of it. And then the almost unthinkable coincidence happened. You too went home between the acts. You called attention to the fact that it was possible; you innocently put the whole scheme in jeopardy."

"But how could he? I didn't waste any time, and he was back and in his seat before me."

"I've heard all about that. But what about leaving for the intermission? Was he in a hurry?"

Her eyes widened. "Why, he left before the curtain. He whispered he had to make a phone call. I didn't think anything of it for he was so busy and hurried that night anyway. And then when intermission time came I went out alone, and tried to phone too. I suppose his saying that gave me the idea. But the one in the lobby was being used, and it took quite a time to find a drug store with an empty one—"

"And by the time you found it Dick had reached your house and killed Jerome."

"But I still don't see how—"

"I didn't for a long time. When I finally got the idea, the police records proved I was right, but it was no wonder they couldn't make the deduction from the record alone. About ten days after the murder a bicycle was picked up from a rack in front of a telegraph office in the block. It was chained to the rack; it had been standing there unclaimed for some days when the boys finally reported it. None of them knew how long it had been there or how it got there. The police took it down to the lost property room and are holding it there still for a claimant."

"But I don't see—"

"What's the fastest way to get through New York City traffic? Watch a telegraph delivery boy some day; they can ride rings around taxicabs. It provided the necessary speed, all right, but it was a risky scheme. A gentleman in evening clothes can't ride a bicycle in the streets of New York without causing comment. He had to have a telegraph boy's cap, and a raincoat to wear over his clothes. And he had to have a bicycle ready in advance, for he couldn't risk being caught in the act of stealing one or even having one reported as missing. So he bought one and put it in the rack a day ahead of time. That was safe enough; every boy would think it belonged to someone else; if anyone noticed there was an extra, he wasn't likely to do anything about it until he had checked up with all the others, made sure there wasn't a new boy, and so on. Dick carried a package to the theater that night, didn't he?"

"Why, yes, he did. It was some new shirts, he said—he carried it from the car without thinking. But how did you know?"

"He had to. There was no other way. There were a raincoat and a cap in that package. He obviously couldn't change to a telegraph boy's uniform. If the night had been so fair that a raincoat would look ridiculous, he'd have had to abandon the scheme for that time."

"You mean, all the time we sat there together he was planning—"

"I do. And before the first act was over, he ducked out one of the emergency exits to the alley, put on the raincoat and the cap, picked up his bicycle, and rode like a man possessed to your apartment. While he was alone in the elevator he had a chance to remove the things. I'm not certain how he got into the apartment, but I presume he must at some time have gotten an impression of your key, for I don't believe he would have chanced ringing the bell when he expected Mrs. Granger to be there."

"He had a key," Doris said. "I gave it to him."

"Never mind. If you hadn't he'd easily have gotten one. This wasn't a thing you could have prevented. He told Jerome some story to explain his presence—that you'd forgotten something, I imagine. For Jerome was obviously not alarmed at his being there. Then he got the gun and shot him. And, by the way, if I'd known as much as I should about guns, I could have put your mind at rest about yourself weeks ago. When you shot your husband under hypnotism, you didn't release the safety catch before you pulled the trigger."

"Would that make any difference?"

"Only that Jerome would be alive now if he'd been shot that way. Dick released it. He must have been upset at not finding Mrs. Granger, but he went ahead. He hadn't allowed himself much time to deal with unexpected contingencies."

"Why wasn't she there, though? What had gone wrong with that?"

"Jerome's the only one who could answer that. He had arranged to move a lamp onto the windowsill when Miss Wright was asleep and the coast clear, as a signal to Mrs. Granger to come upstairs. It seems an awfully juvenile and unnecessarily complicated arrangement with all New York to meet in, but that's what she told me."

"Jerome would like entertaining her at home," Doris said, "and I suppose they had to be careful where they were seen. Tom was jealous."

"Well, whether Betty wouldn't take the drink or something else went wrong, he never put the lamp in the pre-arranged place. Mrs. Granger finally got tired of waiting and came upstairs."

"But she must have come to the door while he was there," Doris said. "I didn't bolt the door when I went in, and Jerome certainly didn't if he was expecting her."

Dr. Owen nodded. "I think so. That must have been a bad moment too, when he heard her at the door. And at about the same instant you began to ring the telephone. It must have seemed that all the furies were after him. Yet he kept his head. Before he went out again he put on the coat and cap; he had to risk meeting her in the lobby, and he hoped that would be disguise enough to get him past her. He didn't meet her as a matter of fact. He pedalled furiously back to the theater, wondering whether the blame would fall now on you or Mrs. Granger. I think he rather hoped it would be the latter."

"And during those last two acts—"

"I don't think that would have been hard for him except for the uncertainty about where you had been. Aside from that, I dare say he enjoyed it."

"And afterwards"—

"I'm perfectly certain, Doris, that he never meant to let you be punished for the murder. He wanted to use insanity as a defense, but the suggestion had to come from someone else. And you kept your head so well that there was never an opportunity for it to come spontaneously. You never faltered; he had to defend you on the basis of your own story."

"But when it was all over—when I was acquitted—he was the one that wanted to go on."

"Vanity—the longing of the murderer to return to the scene of his crime—call it what you like—it's psychopathic under any name. He was certain he'd never be suspected after he'd gone through the trial successfully."

"But then how did you ever happen to suspect him?"

"Miss Pomeroy will tell you I distrusted him from the time I first heard your story. That was a hunch, I suppose. Then when I hypnotized you, the only difference I could discover in what I had said to you the second time was that I'd called him 'Dick' once, and again 'your brother'. You responded to the familiar name by acting out the murder. Every time you went over your story with him he must have been subtly, fiendishly, suggesting the other one, planting it, nurturing it. When I spoke of 'your brother' the less familiar term failed to start the association. I didn't grasp that all at once, but I saw some indication that Dick was intimately connected with your hallucination. The first time I suspected him seriously was when he told me at Keene's office that he didn't know anything about me, and challenged me to say where I'd met you. I'm not precisely famous, but I'm well enough known in the profession that a man who knew how to make inquiries, as Dick certainly should have, could easily have discovered my specialty. When he pretended not to know it, I was suspicious. Your bringing me into the case must have frightened him horribly, Doris. His egocentric mind would jump immediately to the conclusion that you had brought me to watch him."

"And now the thing he dreaded most in all the world has overtaken him—to be shut away from the world—his fine mind to rot in seclusion—why couldn't he have died?"

"It happens to us all, you know. The thing we fear most takes shape and reality from our dread. It was Richard's fear that drove him to murder, and you should know now that the reality will not be so horrible for him as the fear was."

"Yes," she said. "I can understand his committing murder better than his sending me to that place."

"He's been deteriorating rapidly these last few weeks. That trick was bound to be discovered. He made the arrangements in your name and his, explaining that you were coming willingly, but that you were erratic and moody. And then he wrote you that letter and signed my name— he's developed a nice talent for forgery. He threw me off badly with a note in an excellent imitation of your hand about your great-great grandfather's entirely fictitious insanity. But he must have realized that in a few months at the latest the Glenview Lodge outfit would find out something was strange, even if they didn't believe you at first. His only hope of escaping detection there was the possibility you might actually become insane."

"And he tried to kill you so you couldn't get me out?"

"Partly that, and partly because he feared me and my suspicions."

"But then why not Ruth Granger? She knew more than any of us, and she boasted of what she knew."

"Mr. Granger's revenge was her protection. From the time she asked you for that money, she was never out of sight of her husband or one of the servants on the place. Richard did send her a threatening letter that scared her half to death. By the way, you may be pleased to know there's been a reconciliation there."

"No! Ruth and Tom!"

"They have the doctor to thank for it," Miss Pomeroy said. "He had them both in here day before yesterday and talked to them like a Dutch uncle."

Hillis glanced at the nurse, a flickering, whimsical glance, full of affection and self-mockery, and then back at Doris.

"Say it," he invited her. "It's true, I know. I have a talent for interfering in other people's lives that amounts practically to genius. It's not altogether professional; I come by it naturally, and I suppose it's partly the reason I chose the profession I did."

"I wasn't going to say anything of the sort," she denied.

"You're kind," he said. "I guess this is good-bye, Doris.

I've been brutal, I know. It was deliberate. You had to know all this some day, and I never have believed in cutting off a dog's tail by inches. But I can understand the feeling of those ancient kings who used to sentence to death the messengers who brought bad news. That's what I am to you, I know. I hope some day you'll be able to feel a little more kindly toward me."

"I'm grateful," she said.

"Don't be. Don't burden yourself with that. You have some hard months ahead with your mother and your aunt and your child depending on you. Get some rest now, and be ready to face it."

"I'll never be able to get Adriana now. I'm not going to publish the facts you've told me about Dick's heredity. I can do that much at least for him and Aunt Fanny. He's been a brother to me all his life; he's a brother to me now in his misfortune."

"Didn't Miss Pomeroy tell you she is keeping Adriana for you?"

"No—how—where—you did that for me?"

"I did what I would have done for any child if I could. She was in a bad environment, and I helped to take her out of it. She can come back to you at any time."

"Where is she?"

"I'll take you to her if you're sure you're able," Miss Pomeroy said. "Miss Wright that was—Mrs. Mahoney now—is staying with her until you come back. You wouldn't want to upset her again."

"No, of course not. I'll be careful. But now, quickly, please. Oh, Dr. Owen, how can I ever thank you?"

"You can't." He shook his head impatiently. "Go along now with Pomeroy."

The two women hurried down the broad, rubber-paved hospital corridor together.

"Calls himself a psychiatrist," Miss Pomeroy sniffed. "Thinks he can tell people how to run their lives, and he hasn't even got gumption enough to tell the woman he loves that he loves her."

"I know he loves me," Doris said, "but he can't ask me to marry him. Dr. Hillis Owen couldn't marry a woman who's supposed to be Dick's sister."

"Is that what you think?" Miss Pomeroy stopped short. "And him lying there eating his heart out! I'm going back and tell him!"

"No, Miss Pomeroy, you mustn't, you can't, not now!"

"Do you love him?" the older woman asked.

"Yes," Doris answered. "Yes, I do, but—"

"Then you march straight back in there and tell him so," Miss Pomeroy said, "or if you don't, I will."

THE PERENNIAL LIBRARY MYSTERY SERIES

E. C. Bentley

TRENT'S LAST CASE
"One of the three best detective stories ever written."

—Agatha Christie

TRENT'S OWN CASE
"I won't waste time saying that the plot is sound and the detection satisfying. Trent has not altered a scrap and reappears with all his old humor and charm."   —Dorothy L. Sayers

Gavin Black

A DRAGON FOR CHRISTMAS
"Potent excitement!"   —*New York Herald Tribune*

THE EYES AROUND ME
"I stayed up until all hours last night reading *The Eyes Around Me,* which is something I do not do very often, but I was so intrigued by the ingeniousness of Mr. Black's plotting and the witty way in which he spins his mystery. I can only say that I enjoyed the book enormously."

—F. van Wyck Mason

YOU WANT TO DIE, JOHNNY?
"Gavin Black doesn't just develop a pressure plot in suspense, he adds uninfected wit, character, charm, and sharp knowledge of the Far East to make rereading as keen as the first race-through."   —*Book Week*

Nicholas Blake

THE BEAST MUST DIE
"It remains one more proof that in the hands of a really first-class writer the detective novel can safely challenge comparison with any other variety of fiction."   —*The Manchester Guardian*

THE CORPSE IN THE SNOWMAN
"If there is a distinction between the novel and the detective story (which we do not admit), then this book deserves a high place in both categories."   —*The New York Times*

THE DREADFUL HOLLOW
"Pace unhurried, characters excellent, reasoning solid."

—*San Francisco Chronicle*

END OF CHAPTER
". . . admirably solid . . . an adroit formal detective puzzle backed up by firm characterization and a knowing picture of London publishing."
—*The New York Times*

HEAD OF A TRAVELER
"Another grade A detective story of the right old jigsaw persuasion."
—*New York Herald Tribune Book Review*

MINUTE FOR MURDER
"An outstanding mystery novel. Mr. Blake's writing is a delight in itself."
—*The New York Times*

THE MORNING AFTER DEATH
"One of Blake's best."
—Rex Warner

A PENKNIFE IN MY HEART
"Style brilliant . . . and suspenseful."
—*San Francisco Chronicle*

THE PRIVATE WOUND
[Blake's] best novel in a dozen years . . . . An intensely penetrating study of sexual passion . . . . A powerful story of murder and its aftermath."
—Anthony Boucher, *The New York Times*

A QUESTION OF PROOF
"The characters in this story are unusually well drawn, and the suspense is well sustained."
—*The New York Times*

THE SAD VARIETY
"It is a stunner. I read it instead of eating, instead of sleeping."
—Dorothy Salisbury Davis

THE SMILER WITH THE KNIFE
"An extraordinarily well written and entertaining thriller."
—*Saturday Review of Literature*

THOU SHELL OF DEATH
"It has all the virtues of culture, intelligence and sensibility that the most exacting connoisseur could ask of detective fiction."
—*The Times* [London] *Literary Supplement*

THE WHISPER IN THE GLOOM
"One of the most entertaining suspense-pursuit novels in many seasons."
—*The New York Times*

NO TEARS FOR HILDA
"It starts fine and finishes finer. I got behind on breathing watching Max get not only his man but his woman, too."   —Rex Stout

THE RIDDLE OF SAMSON
"The story is an excellent one, the people are quite likable, and the writing is superior."   —*Springfield Republican*

Michael Gilbert

BLOOD AND JUDGMENT
"Gilbert readers need scarcely be told that the characters all come alive at first sight, and that his surpassing talent for narration enhances any plot. . . . Don't miss."   —*San Francisco Chronicle*

THE BODY OF A GIRL
"Does what a good mystery should do: open up into all kinds of ramifications, with untold menace behind the action. At the end, there is a bang-up climax, and it is a pleasure to see how skilfully Gilbert wraps everything up."   —*The New York Times Book Review*

THE DANGER WITHIN
"Michael Gilbert has nicely combined some elements of the straight detective story with plenty of action, suspense, and adventure, to produce a superior thriller."   —*Saturday Review*

DEATH HAS DEEP ROOTS
"Trial scenes superb; prowl along Loire vivid chase stuff; funny in right places; a fine performance throughout."   —*Saturday Review*

FEAR TO TREAD
"Merits serious consideration as a work of art."
          —*The New York Times*

C. W. Grafton

BEYOND A REASONABLE DOUBT
"A very ingenious tale of murder . . . a brilliant and gripping narrative."
          —Jacques Barzun and Wendell Hertig Taylor

Edward Grierson

THE SECOND MAN
"One of the best trial-testimony books to have come along in quite a while."   —*The New Yorker*

Cyril Hare

AN ENGLISH MURDER
"By a long shot, the best crime story I have read for a long time. Everything is traditional, but originality does not suffer. The setting is perfect. Full marks to Mr. Hare."　　　　　　　*—Irish Press*

TRAGEDY AT LAW
"An extremely urbane and well-written detective story."
　　　　　　　　　　　　　　　　—The New York Times

UNTIMELY DEATH
"The English detective story at its quiet best, meticulously underplayed, rich in perceivings of the droll human animal and ready at the last with a neat surprise which has been there all the while had we but wits to see it."　　　　　　*—New York Herald Tribune Book Review*

WHEN THE WIND BLOWS
"The best, unquestionably, of all the Hare stories, and a masterpiece by any standards."
　—Jacques Barzun and Wendell Hertig Taylor, *A Catalogue of Crime*

WITH A BARE BODKIN
"One of the best detective stories published for a long time."
　　　　　　　　　　　　　　　　　　—The Spectator

Matthew Head

THE CABINDA AFFAIR (*available 6/81*)
"An absorbing whodunit and a distinguished novel of atmosphere."
　　　　　　　　—Anthony Boucher, *The New York Times*

MURDER AT THE FLEA CLUB (*available 6/81*)
"The true delight is in Head's style, its limpid ease combined with humor and an awesome precision of phrase."　　*—San Francisco Chronicle*

M. V. Heberden

ENGAGED TO MURDER
"Smooth plotting."　　　　　　　　　　*—The New York Times*

James Hilton

WAS IT MURDER?
"The story is well planned and well written."
　　　　　　　　　　　　　　　　—The New York Times

Thomas Sterling

THE EVIL OF THE DAY
"Prose as witty and subtle as it is sharp and clear...characters unconventionally conceived and richly bodied forth . . . . In short, a novel to be treasured."   —Anthony Boucher, *The New York Times*

Julian Symons

THE BELTING INHERITANCE
"A superb whodunit in the best tradition of the detective story."
                    —August Derleth, *Madison Capital Times*

BLAND BEGINNING
"Mr. Symons displays a deft storytelling skill, a quiet and literate wit, a nice feeling for character, and detectival ingenuity of a high order."
                    —Anthony Boucher, *The New York Times*

BOGUE'S FORTUNE
"There's a touch of the old sardonic humour, and more than a touch of style."   —*The Spectator*

THE BROKEN PENNY
"The most exciting, astonishing and believable spy story to appear in years.   —Anthony Boucher, *The New York Times Book Review*

THE COLOR OF MURDER
"A singularly unostentatious and memorably brilliant detective story."
                    —*New York Herald Tribune Book Review*

THE 31ST OF FEBRUARY
"Nobody has painted a more gruesome picture of the advertising business since Dorothy Sayers wrote 'Murder Must Advertise', and very few people have written a more entertaining or dramatic mystery story."
                    —*The New Yorker*

Dorothy Stockbridge Tillet
(John Stephen Strange)

THE MAN WHO KILLED FORTESCUE
"Better than average."   —*Saturday Review of Literature*

Henry Kitchell Webster

WHO IS THE NEXT? (*available 5/81*)
"A double murder, private-plane piloting, a neat impersonation, and a delicate courtship are adroitly combined by a writer who knows how to use the language."   —Jacques Barzun and Wendell Hertig Taylor

Anna Mary Wells

MURDERER'S CHOICE
"Good writing, ample action, and excellent character work."
—Saturday Review of Literature

A TALENT FOR MURDER
"The discovery of the villain is a decided shock."   *—Books*

**If you enjoyed this book you'll want to know about
THE PERENNIAL LIBRARY MYSTERY SERIES**

Gavin Black

☐	P 473	A DRAGON FOR CHRISTMAS	$1.95
☐	P 485	THE EYES AROUND ME	$1.95
☐	P 472	YOU WANT TO DIE, JOHNNY?	$1.95

George Harmon Coxe

| ☐ | P 527 | MURDER WITH PICTURES | $2.25 |

Edmund Crispin

| ☐ | P 506 | BURIED FOR PLEASURE | $1.95 |

Kenneth Fearing

| ☐ | P 500 | THE BIG CLOCK | $1.95 |

Andrew Garve

☐	P 430	THE ASHES OF LODA	$1.50
☐	P 451	THE CUCKOO LINE AFFAIR	$1.95
☐	P 429	A HERO FOR LEANDA	$1.50
☐	P 449	MURDER THROUGH THE LOOKING GLASS	$1.95
☐	P 441	NO TEARS FOR HILDA	$1.95
☐	P 450	THE RIDDLE OF SAMSON	$1.95

Buy them at your local bookstore or use this coupon for ordering:

HARPER & ROW, Mail Order Dept. #PMS, 10 East 53rd St., New York, N.Y. 10022.
Please send me the books I have checked above. I am enclosing $ _____ which includes a postage and handling charge of $1.00 for the first book and 25¢ for each additional book. Send check or money order. No cash or C.O.D.'s please.

Name _____

Address _____

City _____ State _____ Zip _____
Please allow 4 weeks for delivery. USA and Canada only. This offer expires 1/1/82. Please add applicable sales tax.

Michael Gilbert

☐	P 446	BLOOD AND JUDGMENT	$1.95
☐	P 459	THE BODY OF A GIRL	$1.95
☐	P 448	THE DANGER WITHIN	$1.95
☐	P 447	DEATH HAS DEEP ROOTS	$1.95
☐	P 458	FEAR TO TREAD	$1.95

C. W. Grafton

☐	P 519	BEYOND A REASONABLE DOUBT	$1.95

Edward Grierson

☐	P 528	THE SECOND MAN	$2.25

Cyril Hare

☐	P 455	AN ENGLISH MURDER	$1.95
☐	P 522	TRAGEDY AT LAW	$2.25
☐	P 514	UNTIMELY DEATH	$1.95
☐	P 454	WHEN THE WIND BLOWS	$1.95
☐	P 523	WITH A BARE BODKIN	$2.25

Matthew Head

☐	P 541	THE CABINDA AFFAIR (available 6/81)	$2.25
☐	P 542	MURDER AT THE FLEA CLUB (available 6/81)	$2.25

Buy them at your local bookstore or use this coupon for ordering:

HARPER & ROW, Mail Order Dept. #PMS, 10 East 53rd St., New York, N.Y. 10022.

Please send me the books I have checked above. I am enclosing $ _____ which includes a postage and handling charge of $1.00 for the first book and 25¢ for each additional book. Send check or money order. No cash or C.O.D.'s please.

Name _____

Address _____

City _____ State _____ Zip _____

Please allow 4 weeks for delivery. USA and Canada only. This offer expires 1/1/82. Please add applicable sales tax.

M. V. Heberden

☐ P 533   ENGAGED TO MURDER $2.25

James Hilton

☐ P 501   WAS IT MURDER? $1.95

Elspeth Huxley

☐ P 540   THE AFRICAN POISON MURDERS
         (available 5/81) $2.25

Frances Iles

☐ P 517   BEFORE THE FACT $1.95
☐ P 532   MALICE AFORETHOUGHT $1.95

Lange Lewis

☐ P 518   THE BIRTHDAY MURDER $1.95

Arthur Maling

☐ P 482   LUCKY DEVIL $1.95
☐ P 483   RIPOFF $1.95
☐ P 484   SCHROEDER'S GAME $1.95

Austin Ripley

☐ P 387   MINUTE MYSTERIES $1.95

Buy them at your local bookstore or use this coupon for ordering:

Thomas Sterling

☐ P 529 THE EVIL OF THE DAY $2.25

Julian Symons

☐ P 468 THE BELTING INHERITANCE $1.95
☐ P 469 BLAND BEGINNING $1.95
☐ P 481 BOGUE'S FORTUNE $1.95
☐ P 480 THE BROKEN PENNY $1.95
☐ P 461 THE COLOR OF MURDER $1.95
☐ P 460 THE 31ST OF FEBRUARY $1.95

Dorothy Stockbridge Tillet
(John Stephen Strange)

☐ P 536 THE MAN WHO KILLED FORTESCUE $2.25

Henry Kitchell Webster

☐ P 539 WHO IS THE NEXT? (available 5/81) $2.25

Anna Mary Wells

☐ P 534 MURDERER'S CHOICE $2.25
☐ P 535 A TALENT FOR MURDER $2.25

Buy them at your local bookstore or use this coupon for ordering: